THE GREAT AND AWFUL SUMMER

mitzi dale

NIMBUS
PUBLISHING

Author's note: I am indebted to: Penelope Jackson, editor; Frank McEnaney, mentor.

Acknowledgements: *Wuthering Heights*, by Emily Brontë; *Cape Breton Lives*, edited by Ron Caplan; *Wind, Whales and Whisky*, by Silver Donald Cameron; Howard & Debbie MacKinnon, Knotty Pine Cottages, Cape Breton; Jocelyne Marchan, Marchandise, Grand Pré, Nova Scotia.

Nimbus Publishing Limited
PO Box 9166, Halifax, NS B3K 5M8
(902) 455-4286

Printed and bound in Canada

Design: Co. & Co. Design
Author photo: John Knox

Library and Archives Canada Cataloguing in Publication

    Dale, Mitzi, 1956-
    The great and awful summer / Mitzi Dale.
    ISBN 978-1-55109-614-8 ISBN 10: 1-55109-614-5
    I. Title.

PS8557.A453G74 2007   jC813'.54   C2007-902421-1

We acknowledge the financial support of the Government of Canada through the Book Publishing Industry Development Program (BPIDP) and the Canada Council, and of the Province of Nova Scotia through the Department of Tourism, Culture and Heritage for our publishing activities.

to

Monica, Blair & Gillian

ONE

HELP WANTED

CC Lodge, Rough Cove, Cape Breton
This rustic family-oriented resort still has
openings for the following:
• Wait Staff (experience preferred but not
  necessary)
• Busboy/girl (no experience necessary)
• Daycare staff (a love of kids required)

JUST LOOKING AT THAT AD made my stomach
go twisty. Oh, man, I wanted a job at CC Lodge. I
was at that age when my parents couldn't just park
me in an arts camp anymore while they got on with
their lives, and I was still too young to get on with
my own. That's how it felt then, anyway. I now
realize that every mundane millisecond I've spent
on this earth is my Life, but that year felt like being
on hold.

"Sarah Leanne Lockwood? Press One for your
Life. We're sorry, all lines are busy just now, but
your call means a great deal to us. Please hold to

maintain priority sequence and a Life representative will be with you shortly."

The perfect age to get a summer job. I'd heard about CC Lodge from my best friend's older sister who'd worked there and said it was too awesome for mere words to describe and then proceeded to talk about it for half an hour after all. At the time the place sounded scary to me because of the owners, Cathy and Cliff (hence the CC).

"Cathy is sooo nice and Cliff is sooo hot."

That had been enough to gross me out right there. I was only ten after all. Plus, she said, Cathy and Cliff gave the teenagers on the staff a ton of freedom—as long as you did your job well, your time was your own—and the stories of partying and boys grossed me out even more. But the second I saw that ad the formerly scary monologue came back to me practically word for word and I got all excited and very superstitious.

I sat down immediately and wrote a letter. By hand. That was the first of the superstitions. The letter had to be handwritten. The ad gave no email address anyway, and from the things my best friend's sister had said it was clear that Cathy and Cliff liked "real" people so I didn't even send a computer printout. What could be more real than your own handwriting? Even though I'd had only babysitting experience my letter was basically an essay about my attitude towards kids and what I would do, and mostly would not do, with them. On the last page I neatly printed the same three references I always use: my favourite teacher, the parents of the girl I babysit for most often, and a neighbour who pays me to go into her house and water her plants when she visits her son out west.

The second superstition was that I had to mail this application without telling anybody. Just letting one person know what I was up to might dissipate the energy waves I was sending out. This was especially difficult as my mum had started doing her have-you-thought-abouts.

"Have you thought about this, Sarah?"

Then I'd look at what she was pointing to and it would be a homemade poster with the little phone numbers you can rip off the bottom. One of the ads she showed me was for volunteering to visit old folks and one was for an actual paid job walking someone's dog. No, thanks.

The third superstition was that the application letter shouldn't be folded. I imagined a huge bag of mail being dumped at the lodge and my big brown envelope standing out in the pile so they'd reach for it first.

Though I wouldn't recommend giving any prospective employers a handwritten essay to read, they must have decided I was all right, because

I got the job without even having to go for an interview! Well, it would have been pretty hard to go for an interview, since I live in New Brunswick. And when I think about it now, my friend's big sister had said that one of the great things about the job was that kids came to work there from all over Canada and the United States. Here I was picturing in my mind C and C being wowed by me in person after my great handwritten letter, when in fact all that happened was that after two weeks of beaming out energy waves, I got a reply saying I'd been hired. There was a map enclosed showing how to get there and a photocopied list of things I might want to bring with me. Reality, at least until that summer, has always been a lot less dramatic than what goes on in my head.

My mum was immediately devastated. Me not telling anyone I'd applied and then suddenly saying I was working at CC Lodge for the summer caught her off guard.

"You'll be gone for the whole summer?"

"It's just a day's drive," my dad put in. "We can visit. We'll camp. It'll be fun."

"What about *Willow Heights*?"

Oh, god, I'm embarrassed at how this momentarily did give me pause. *Willow Heights* is the juiciest soap opera in the world and my mum and I are both addicted, and this is too embarrassing, because I have school when it's on so she tapes it and we watch it together in one gorge-fest on Sunday morning while the rest of the world sleeps in or golfs or washes cars or does whatever normal people do. We even take a tray with tea and muffins down to the basement so we don't have to come upstairs for anything.

"Ellis Bell is falling in love with Hermione Rushworth. I know he is."

Just saying the name "Ellis" gave me shivers. Of course, that isn't his real name, that's his soap name. His real name is Edgar Linton, which doesn't suit him at all. Now, my mum's been watching the show for years and she says that when he started, Ellis Bell was a bad guy—he'd actually served time for something, I don't know what—but the audience liked him so much that the scriptwriters made it so that he'd been framed and his record was cleared and he got out and completed his medical studies and became a humble family doctor so that he could help people. He is so gorgeous and his wife is so mean—Arabella Guring, the spoiled daughter of the richest man in town—but he's faithful to her because he understands that she's just like that because of the way she was raised. Everyone in Willow Heights hates her but they're afraid of her and we're always hoping that Ellis Bell will divorce her and marry the also rich but kind socialite, Hermione, who spends so much of her time volunteering, especially at WHGH (Willow Heights General Hospital). She was the only one who would even go near Mark the high school teacher when he got AIDS—

Oh my god, I'm telling the plot of a soap opera. That's how addictive it is.

Start again.

My dad was all keen on my getting the job because a) dads don't take your going away personally and b) he really did want to go camping. He'd camped a lot as a kid himself and had all these fond memories of fishing and cookouts and hunting, but since neither my mum nor my sister nor I were at all into fishing and hunting he'd never gotten around to it as an adult. That didn't stop us from giving him camping-related things for birthdays and Father's Day, though. Most dads get socks and handkerchiefs and ties, right? Our dad gets clever camping gear. He has a set of nesting pots—small, larger, largest—and they fit inside each other so neatly, including the handles which can turn a hundred and eighty degrees, that they appear to be a single giant measuring cup when you look at them from eye level. Years ago we bought a dome tent that came with a little side tent attached so that kids can sleep separately from parents. My sister and I used to set it up in the back yard and use it as a playhouse. The purchase of the gas stove one Christmas meant that for several years after that we could buy him clever packages of unusual dried food—everything from cauliflower curry to chocolate cake. Just add water, stir, and pour into one of the stacking pots and you've got a fancy meal out under the stars. Then there was the Swiss Army knife, the bivvy sack, the mosquito net and the waterproofed everythings. Waterproofed matches, ponchos, flashlights, first aid kits. We all enjoyed shopping for my dad but no one ever wanted to go camping with him.

Now, thanks to me and my summer job, he'd have the opportunity.

WE GOT UP EARLY the morning before I was supposed to start the job. My dad had packed the car the night before and, what with all the camping gear, there wasn't that much room left in the trunk for my stuff so I had to have it in the back seat with me. I was happy to have my pillow since I was only half awake and I fell back to sleep pretty soon after we hit the highway. We had just grabbed a quick piece of toast for breakfast because we'd planned to have breakfast at the Big Stop at the border between New Brunswick and Nova Scotia. It had seemed like a good plan the night before but it's a long drive and by the time we got there I was wide awake and all three of us were starved. This being Canada Day long weekend, the restaurant was just packed. We ate a huge brunch and sat there for a long time because we realized that once we got back in the car we were seriously on our way to my summer job. My mum bravely tried to pretend she was getting into the idea.

"I'm looking forward to the Cabot Trail," she said. "I haven't driven it since I was a little girl."

You know those trips you take with your parents and your mum asks every half hour if she should take over the driving and your dad says, no, he'll let her know if he gets tired and they're always trying to get you to look up from your magazine (or DVD if you're lucky) to see The View? Then when you finally do look up at The View it's not even that great but unless you make some comment about it they won't believe you were really looking? It was like that. For hours. Only I have to confess that once we crossed the causeway between Nova Scotia and Cape Breton my stomach did start to get twisty. Not because of The View—one side looked pretty much like the other to me—but because I was thinking, *This is it. I'm on an island and I'm going to be here, alone, for almost two whole months.*

It was scary, and I was getting myself all stirred up over it when my dad's announcement broke through.

"Ladies and gentlemen, we are now entering the Cabot Trail."

You know what? My mind was taken off my panic by The View. We drove and drove and up ahead we could see the road—a pale, twisting line against the green forests—curving up and back on itself, and I remember thinking, *Is that where we're going to be going?* And in a few minutes we'd be *there*, at the point that had seemed impossible to reach only moments before. I wish there were a poem about it somewhere because all we could say was that it was beautiful.

"Beautiful," Mum said.

"It's so beautiful," I said.

"Spectacularly beautiful," Dad said.

I mean, you're driving along hugging the shore, so there's water on one side of the car and these big rounded mountains are plunging at you from the other side. Every turn, and there are plenty, seems to take you to a whole new place—farmland, fishing village, wild forest—you just never know what to expect around the bend.

Now, here's the thing about islands. We'd been driving all day in sunshine and cloudless skies, but as soon as we'd crossed over to Cape Breton there were clouds, and that meant that as we drove along, and the clouds moved in front of the sun, the wooded mountains appeared different shades of green.

"Beautiful."

"So beautiful."

"Here we go," Dad said.

There was a green-and-white sign saying, "You are now at the base of Smokey: You will climb 221m–725 ft." I looked up and saw the most amazing curved-back-on-itself bend yet, and a few minutes later when we reached that bend I sucked in my breath.

"Whoa!"

It actually made my stomach churn to be so high up and suddenly facing wide open ocean on a tight bend like that. My mum said it was getting to her, too.

My dad was loving it.

When we were turned away from the ocean and heading down again, the most amazing cloud was rolling over the mountain.

"Guess that's why they call it Smokey," my dad said.

"You think?"

"Of course."

I said "rolling," not "hanging," because even as we descended from our last turn the cloud spread about halfway down the mountain. It was like watching time-lapse photography.

"What happened to our great weather?" my mum asked.

Raindrops were starting to hit the windshield.

"How much farther to the park?" my dad asked.

Mum always navigated. Our plan was to go past Rough Cove, set up camp at the national park, then backtrack and explore a bit to find out exactly where CC Lodge was.

"Feel that?" my dad asked.

The wind was really buffeting the car and he'd had to jerk it back from drifting over to the other side of the road. Mum looked up from the map.

"This is Ingonish Ferry," she said. "We're close—stop!"

My dad pulled over suddenly.

"What's wrong?"

"Nothing."

"Nothing?"

My dad gets a little tense when the driving is difficult.

"I'm sorry, Honey, it's just…I thought I saw a Vacancy sign back there. Knotty Pine Cottages."

We sat in silence in the car while the wind blew and the rain started falling more heavily. My dad didn't even bother pointing out that he had waterproofed everythings in the trunk because who wants to set up a tent in the driving wind and rain? It was a no-brainer—forget camping.

Twenty minutes later we were warm and cozy and my mum was heating up chilli on the little stove in the cabin instead of on the gas stove outdoors. Our cabin had a balcony and, if the weather had been good enough to see anything, A View. There was a tiny TV but when we turned it on we could hardly see anything, the reception was so bad.

My parents fell asleep as soon as their heads hit the pillow, but for the longest time I lay awake in the bed beside them listening to the wind and the rain. At one point I got up and looked outside, but it was pitch black and all I could see was the silhouette of a nearby birch tree bending wildly in the wind. Except for a ten-day visit to my grandma when I was eight, this would be my longest time away from home.

THREE

CAPE BRETON BY MORNING was a lot less dramatic than Cape Breton by night. Less dramatic, but with the sun and sea and drifts of cloud overhead it was every bit as beautiful. Our cabin view looked across a tidal inlet. When I held my hands up to my eyes like blinkers to contain the scene it seemed that we were on one side of a pretty little lake and just across the way houses and cabins like the one we were staying in dotted the landscape. Turning my head slightly to the right and keeping my hands up, I could create another view entirely. Ocean, sky, and nothing else. When I took my hands away my brain still wanted to choose between the small scene and the big scene, like that optical illusion where you have to choose between seeing an old witch or a beautiful woman.

"Not bad for your first job, Sarah."

My dad had brought his coffee out onto the balcony.

"My first summer job was in a lumber mill."

He sipped at his coffee.

"According to the map they sent us you're going to be just around that point."

He gestured across the inlet to where the lake scene met the ocean scene. Just over there, barely five minutes away by car, was the place I'd be spending the next two months.

"Excited?" my dad asked.

"Nervous," I said.

"It's often the same thing. Let's go eat."

My mum had made my favourite breakfast, French toast with lots of cinnamon and maple syrup. We did our dishes, packed the car, and headed out.

In order to keep me from being too nervous and my mum from being too mushy my dad started singing "She'll be comin' 'round Mount Smokey when she comes," and by the time I was having to "sleep with grandma" we were rounding the point and I looked back across the inlet and could see the very group of cabins where we'd spent the night. When I faced forward again there was an entirely new scene in front of me: waves crashing against big black rocks that jutted up like sea-stacks. Once the waves had crashed, the water pulled back to reveal more black rocks, smoother ones that clustered around the base of the jagged ones.

Again the trail curved tightly back towards the mountains and in moments we were turning onto a dirt road and driving under a sign that said CC

Lodge. The parking lot was surrounded by trees, but not so thickly that we couldn't get glimpses of the lodge and the ocean. A dark red building nearby had a carved sign saying simply "Office" above the door. No sooner were we out of the car than a woman emerged from the office that I immediately knew must be Cathy. She wore a long skirt with a loose long-sleeved top and no makeup.

"You must be Sarah," she said. "I'm Cathy. Welcome aboard."

My parents had just introduced themselves when a woman came up to Cathy with a problem.

"This is Arvi," Cathy said. "She's, well, she's much more than our chef, she's my right-hand woman…could this wait, Arvi? I'd like to show Sarah and her parents around."

By the furrow in Arvi's brow I didn't think the problem could wait and obviously neither did Cathy.

"Where's Cate?" Cathy asked.

"I last saw her in the dining room."

"I'll join you in the office soon, Arvi. I'll get Cate to show the Lockwoods around."

Arvi headed for the office.

"Cate's our daughter," Cathy said as she started walking. "She's the same age as you, Sarah."

We were on a path about as wide as a sidewalk, me and Cathy together and my mum and dad behind. We soon emerged from the trees and then we had a view of the whole place. There was a big building that caught my attention first; it was the main lodge. The path we were on led right to it, but there were little footpaths branching off to the left and right and Cathy told me that they led to the wharf and the guest cabins. On the wharf there was a rack that held three kayaks, and tied to the wharf were a couple of wooden boats with "CC Lodge" painted on them.

Most of the cabins where guests stayed were smaller than the one we'd rented the night before and they didn't have kitchenettes or balconies, but there were three that were larger and fancier. Cathy said that people who rented the larger ones tended to stay for longer than one week. All the buildings were grouped in a higgledy-piggledy fashion in order to be in keeping with the surroundings, Cathy said, and for that reason they were also painted different colours.

"Cliff feels very strongly that we should maintain the integrity of the place," Cathy said, "so all of the buildings were either built by him or moved here. The office, for instance, was moved here. It was our childhood home."

Her childhood home? It wasn't much bigger than my bedroom! I guess I couldn't keep the surprised look off my face.

"Oh, yes, things were different in those days."

"Simpler times," my dad said.

"Harder times," said my mum.

Cathy chuckled.

"You sound like me and Cliff. I'm always pushing for just a little more comfort for the guests and he's always resisting it."

She turned to me. "You have Cliff to thank for the fact that there's no TV, and that to access the internet you'll have to use the public C@P Site at Gar Harbour."

No TV? Not even for DVDs or videos? My dad had a big grin on his face, the bum.

"And you have me to thank for the fact that the food is out of this world," Cathy said. "If Cliff had his way we'd scrve chowder and brown bread every night."

She turned to my mum. "Arvi is such a find." Apparently Arvi spent half the year in France with her sisters and the other half in Cape Breton helping Cathy and Cliff with CC Lodge. "The one bone of contention now is the porta-potties," Cathy said. I hadn't noticed any porta-potties. "Cliff can't stand them and wants outhouses, but the plan is to eventually build the staff their own showers and washrooms up there." She pointed to some woods on the side of the lodge opposite the ocean, but I couldn't see anything but trees. "We're hoping to start building this September. Until then, I like the fact that they're delivered in the spring and taken away in the fall." She turned to me. "That doesn't help staff this year, I'm afraid, so you'll have to use the same showers as the customers down here."

By then we were at the main lodge. Cathy said that was where all the cooking was done, where everyone ate their meals, and where they held bingo games and ceilidhs. Cate wasn't there, though.

My parents picked up on the fact that Cathy really wanted to get back to Arvi, even though she was being very nice to us and making us feel welcome, so they suggested that we all walk her back to the office and they'd be on their way. We met a girl on the walk back.

"Hey, Marsha," Cathy said, "have you seen Cate?"

Apparently, Marsha had last seen Cate out walking on the road.

"She's supposed to be prepping for lunch."

"Maybe she's back by now…that was a while ago."

There were goodbyes and well wishes and Cathy disappeared into the office and my parents took my stuff out of the car and gave me hugs and kisses and I think we were all glad that Marsha was standing there waiting to give me the rest of the tour because it meant that we couldn't drag the parting scene out too long.

The rest of the tour was the best part. We took a path that veered away from the ocean toward the pond. It was fed by a lovely little waterfall and it had a teeny tiny beach that had been created by trucking in sand. There were kids splashing in the pond and mums sitting nearby reading paperbacks. Beyond that, tucked out of the way in the woods between the lodge and the Cabot Trail, were the cabins where the staff stayed. That's where I saw the first porta-potty.

"Yeah," Marsha said, "it's a drag to have to use the same shower as the guests, but that's life. And this," she said, pointing to where the footpath led off to the right, "leads back to the office. So you'll have gone full circle, see?"

We started down that path and the trees thinned out a little so that I could see through to the office and the parking lot. I stopped in front of a tiny building made of wooden shingles.

"What's this?" I asked. It looked liked the oldest building on the property.

"This," Marsha said, "is the old ice house. It's just used for storage now."

She flung open the door.

"Oh, I'm sorry," she said and shut it quickly.

"Yeah, so, anyway," she continued in a loud voice as though she meant to be heard by whoever she'd seen inside, "in the old days they used to keep blocks of ice in there covered in sawdust. Now it's just used for storage. Let's go find out which cabin you'll be staying in."

As we emerged into the parking lot again I wasn't really listening to Marsha. My mind was on what she'd seen going on in that ice house. I decided there were some kids making out in there, but once again, my imagination had gotten a little carried away with me and it wasn't like that at all.

Marsha spotted Cathy walking quickly and called out to her. Instead of just waiting for us to catch up to her, Cathy came towards us.

"Cate's back," Marsha said. "She's in the ice house."

"Thank you, Marsha," Cathy said. Then she turned to me. "Well, what do you think of the place?"

"Awesome," I said.

And I meant it. Even though I keep calling it a resort it didn't look the way you think of a resort, with swimming pools and spas and all of that. It looked more like a place where a bunch of people had decided to build their little cottages. I told her that.

"Good," Cathy said. "Cliff will like to hear that."

Then she was off on the footpath that led to the ice house.

As time went on I would become aware of the fact that Cathy, though she seemed so easygoing and calm, was in fact always on the move, checking in with the guests, the staff, ordering this, signing for that. Somehow she managed to do all that and still take the time to make someone like me feel welcome. That very night, for instance, she was planning to have an orientation cookout for those of us who were new.

I couldn't wait.

FOUR

THE TIDE WAS OUT and after the cookout we made a big bonfire down on the stony beach. Some of the guys dragged big driftwood logs to sit on and some of the girls had brought camp chairs. We couldn't use the chairs that were for guests because they were all made of wood and it would have been quite a performance to carry them down there. But with the driftwood, a bench, and the camp chairs and everybody getting up to stretch or poke at the fire and moving around a bit it all worked out.

There were a couple of other university students, like Marsha, who'd been there since May or June, and now we high school students had arrived for the peak months of July and August. Cliff wasn't there, but Cate was. She sat with her hands shoved into her windbreaker, staring into the fire. Every now and then Cathy would catch her eye and make little head movements as if to say, "Go introduce yourself," but Cate just kept staring into the fire. I was gearing up to go say hi and introduce myself—and, oh, how I wish I had—when the game started.

Cathy had organized an icebreaker to introduce the new staff. Just the word "game" conjures up stupid stuff, but this was the kind I love, where you really just sit around and talk. She passed around a salad bowl with a whole bunch of folded bits of paper in it and everyone had to pick a piece and not open it up until it was their turn. The idea was not to think too much but just say the first thing that popped into your head.

The first to go was a boy named Todd from Maine, who looked about thirteen but was actually fifteen. He opened his bit of paper.

"Your worst fear," he read aloud. "That's easy. Having to go first in this game."

That got a laugh, but then he said that, seriously, his worst fear was publicly humiliating himself like, for instance, spilling coffee in someone's lap or knocking their heads with a tray when he went to the kitchen. That got one of the university students reminiscing about how just the other day she'd been carrying a big bowl of fettuccine to a table of ten people and, whoosh, it had all fallen forward onto the floor. Another waiter was there in a moment with two of those little brown plastic trays to scoop the whole mess up practically before she'd had time to register what had happened. Then someone else came and mopped up and before she knew it she was carrying out another bowl of fettuccine—*very* carefully—and everything was fine.

"Everybody helps everybody else," she said. "We've all screwed up before."

By the time it came around to me we were getting pretty good at just saying the first thing that popped into our heads, so I opened up the folded paper.

"What would you want to take to a desert island?" I read aloud, and my response was immediate.

"Dental floss."

Think about it. You can wash yourself in the sea and rub palm leaves over your teeth, but if you're living on stringy things like mango and coconut you'd go insane if you couldn't get the bits out, right? So that very night I was assumed to be some sort of clean freak or something, which I am certainly not (and this became apparent to everyone very quickly because I let my side of the cabin deteriorate) it's just that I can't stand that pressure between the teeth or having my tongue constantly going to the same spot and working away at it. And I personally find it very satisfying to see the little bitsy thing that felt so huge in my mouth hanging from the floss afterwards.

See, now I'm justifying myself but there's no need to do that because you're supposed to say the first thing that pops into your head and there's no good or bad answer anyway. Except that for the rest of the summer dental floss became a kind of theme.

For instance, I love vermicelli noodles and I was thrilled when Arvi planned meals with vermicelli rice noodles because I can't get enough of them, but then Jason from Ontario said that dinner looked like a bowl of dental floss (okay, he actually said dental floss with vomit on it—guys!) and it was all ha ha, very funny, except that once he'd said it even I had trouble looking at my rice noodles. Took about two weeks to get over it. And every now and then I'd find one of those little circular travel-sized flosses under my soup bowl or some wacky flavour like cinnamon. Perhaps I went too far at the bonfire telling them that my personal favourite floss was the mint-flavoured, waxed, thicker, thready kind— though definitely not as thick as the dental tape. Anyway, the joke went on and on. It didn't help that when my mother sent me my first care package (and she actually wrote Care Package on the outside) it contained, in addition to three different varieties of sun block—SPF 45, 30, and 15, scented, unscented and sport—and the first installment of the *Willow Heights* updates, my favourite floss.

There I go again. None of this matters.

Okay, but I do have to get off my chest the fact that one thing that really bugs me is those little floss "sticks" that they sell. They're plastic with a lethal tail end, which I suppose is meant to act like a toothpick, and the teeny tiny bit of floss you get is strung across the two plastic prongs and they may be useful to some people for the front teeth but you can forget doing your molars—

Start again.

The game, yes, it wasn't as bad as it sounds. I'll never forget when Tara, who turned out to be one of my roommates, picked out her piece of paper and read "best piece of advice you've ever received," and right away went into a story about how her mum said that when she was at a meeting once, and was getting irritated with everyone trying to have her own way, she just suddenly saw all the women as little girls at a tea party and it cooled her down. The sharp-tongued one in the red suit with shoulder pads was like a little Lucy figure from *Peanuts*, bossing everyone around, stuff like that. I liked that. I could tell Cathy liked it too because I saw her nodding with a little smile on her face. Tara was pretty and she wore her hair shorter than any of the boys. She didn't feel she had to be yuck yuck funny all the time, but she wasn't a party pooper either. Earthy, I guess, which is apparently what her name means.

The only person who refused to take a piece of paper from the bowl was Cate. Now, that didn't strike me as too big a deal at the time, because I get tired of my parents' stuff, too. My dad always has little quotes for every occasion and my mum makes us play charades every Christmas, so I could relate. At first I found it a little odd when I heard that she was going to room with us instead of in her parents' house, where she lived the rest of the year, but then even that wasn't so weird, really. I mean, who wouldn't rather spend a summer in a cabin with a bunch of girls than stuck in the house with the folks? When the bowl was handed to her she just took it and passed it to a girl beside her called Ellen.

Ellen was the oldest of the high school kids and not at all shy because her family had moved around so much when she was young. She did a whole funny riff about names that first night. Except for the boys, who were all in one large and, by the end of the summer, incredibly stinky cabin, we were assigned sleeping arrangements randomly (names in a bowl) and it just so happened that we ended up in the following arrangement: Brittany, Hilary, Bethany; and Cate, Tara, Ellen, me. Ellen immediately started a routine about what all of us would soon be calling the BHB girls.

"Row, row, row your boat, Brittany along, Hilary, Hilary, Bethany, Bethany, Life is but a song."

Whenever I hear that tune now, I sing "Hilary, Hilary, Bethany, Bethany" in my head.

"*Our* names," meaning the four of us in our cabin, "are reactions to the ones ahead of *us*," Ellen continued. "You know, like, Laser Moonbeam Sunset and Honest Wild Milkweed."

"Honest Wild Milkweed?"

"Whatever. Poor munchkins now are gettin' last names for first names—I know, like, a Landon, a Hunter, and a MacKenzie." Pause. "Those are the *girls.*"

Ellen was from California, she was a riot, and she talked in italics. But she was smart enough to know that Tara meant "earthy," and she said her and my names were grandma names (true!). She said she was thinking of doing her name backwards, because Nelle was more interesting, and then she said maybe Tara could change hers to White Oaks and I didn't get it so they had to explain that Tara was the name of Scarlett O'Hara's plantation in *Gone With the Wind* and I think she was just about to launch into a rendition of "Que Sarah, Sarah" for me when Cate cut her off.

"Spare us," she said.

We knew by the way she said it that she wasn't joking. Also, it was the first thing she'd said to any of us all night.

So right away Ellen and Cate were, ahem, somewhat at odds. Once the initial shock of being shot down was over, and the bowl was being passed around again, Ellen leaned over and whispered in my ear.

"Just like *her* name, huh? Short and sharp."

Now, who knows if that was what she was really like or if she got off on the wrong foot with us that night and that set the tone for the rest of her time? I'd sure like to know. There was such a nice friendly feeling around that fire that it did seem like Cate had some kind of chip on her shoulder. At the time I wanted to bop her on the head for being such a downer, but now I'd like to go back and freeze that moment and find some way to relate to her. Maybe if I could have had some little alarm bell go off in my head—"troubled person here"—and reacted in some way *for* her instead of *to* her, then the rest of the summer would have been completely different and I wouldn't have this awful guilty feeling now.

But I didn't. And now I want a second (and third and fourth) chance.

FIVE

WHAT DID I WANT from that summer? Too much, I guess. Admittedly part of me just wanted something exciting to happen, anything, even if it meant a spaceship landing and inviting me to be their Earth sample. I'd have gone! And the thing about fantasies is that they do come true, sort of—my getting this job at CC Lodge was a fantasy that had come true—but it doesn't turn out exactly the way you fantasize about it, ever. I guess it can't. I guess because fantasies have a beginning, middle, and end (that's what I like about them), and real life goes on and on and on. In real life, the happy ending disintegrates and something else starts up again.

For instance, I had the opportunity in grade seven to act out a *Willow Heights* fantasy. I'd just recently gotten hooked on the show and at night I'd put myself to sleep with the thought of the opening credits: "starring Sarah Leanne Lockwood."

The real *Willow Heights* opens with a shot of an amazing stand of willows. At first we're far away as the credits roll and the theme music swells, then we zoom zoom zoom until we're right in among the swaying leaves and for the final credits we're smack up against the bark of the biggest old leaning tree. In my pre-sleep routine I'm new to Willow Heights—I've just moved from the city—and I'm out of place being not only a poet but always dressed in black. So I take to solitary evening strolls out to the willows and I move into them even slower than the camera does and I'm leaning against a big trunk, having my sad poetic thoughts, when I become aware that someone else is inside the swaying streaming circle—Ellis Bell! Of course, as I'm new to town I haven't a clue who he is. I even experience a momentary irritation that anyone else is in my willow circle at all. That goes away, though, when I realize that this guy is very handsome and also, I suspect, a little sad like me.

The fantasy never got much further than that in grade seven because I always fell asleep with the leaves swishing and Ellis looking at me with longing, but during the summer my best friend Pam and I had a sleepover at her house and we decided to sneak out and meet our boyfriends—this was a piece of cake to do because we slept in the trailer in her driveway—and the place we were to meet them was under the willow tree a few streets over!

It was very exciting waiting in the trailer with Pam. And sneaking out by moonlight and walking around. Every time a car or even a cat went by our stomachs went all twisty. But when we got to our secret meeting place half of the willows had been trimmed to prevent the leaves from dripping onto the road, so the whole stand looked like a mastodon with blunt cut bangs.

Also, and I feel bad about this now, I didn't really care much about my boyfriend, I just wanted to have one and he was Pam's boyfriend's best friend so we sort of hung out in a foursome anyway. I don't even remember kissing him that night but I do remember leaning back against the willow tree and closing my eyes and the ripply bark was really uncomfortable on my shoulder blades.

When we got back to the trailer, it was clear that Pam had had a great time.

"Isn't it wonderful having a boy's strong arms around you?"

She actually said that. She clearly had no fantasy about branches wreathing around her, the whole experience was just what it was—sneak out, make out, sneak back—and so there was no disappointment. Nothing had disintegrated for her. Oh well. I still wouldn't give up my fantasies, because it can also go the other way—real life turns out even better—and besides, you get to practice how you would handle different situations.

Now that I've had the experience of Cate, for

instance, in my mind I practice meeting someone who seems sharp tongued and unfriendly and instead of writing her off I put on my least annoying face and say, "Are you feeling okay today?" Then she spills her guts and I'm totally understanding and she feels great for having gotten her problems off her chest and when I'm an old lady lying in bed reading magazines I see an article by this famous person I don't recognize and she's talking about the time she'd been so down she was actually contemplating suicide but a complete stranger, Sarah Leanne Lockwood, someone she'd only met once but had never forgotten since, had understood her misery and listened and since that day she'd never looked back but had gone on to...climb Mount Everest, cure cancer or win the Oscar.

I do go on, don't I?

Actually, there's more. I smile as I think of all the people I've saved just by being my simple kind self and I close my eyes and literally fall into a dead sleep. Sometimes I even go so far as to imagine the letters about me in the newspaper, or my funeral where my family is astounded by the number of strangers who show up to pay their respects. Ellen calls this morbid. I call it practice.

SIX

ONE OF THE BEST PARTS of that summer was the job itself. I loved being with the munchkins. Maybe it's because I never had any little brothers or sisters to take care of or something, but I just think they're so cute. Whenever I babysit, as soon as the parents have left I immediately get down on the floor at kid level. If they're really little I even lie down and let them crawl all over me. With some kids it takes a while, but eventually they all come to check you out because it's irresistible.

The very first day on this job felt a little strange, though, because suddenly there were nine little people looking at me as if to say, "What now?" In that moment of terror (*what now?*) an idea popped into my head. Why not all make individual t-shirts at the beginning of our week together? There was a store within walking distance that printed designs on clothes and I figured they'd have fabric paint or crayons too, which they did, thank heavens.

Anyway, it's not the kind of idea you can follow through on without support from the higher ups so I gathered my crew and had us all hold hands while we searched for one of the Cs. We found Cliff first. This was the first time I'd actually seen him, so I had to introduce myself. I left the kids playing Ring Around a Rosie while I approached him with my plan. He was chopping wood.

"Excuse me?" I said.

Two pieces of wood split off in opposite directions and the axe hit the stump. He didn't reach for another log but stopped chopping and looked at me. I remembered my friend's big sister's words and thought this couldn't be Cliff because she'd said he was hot. This guy had black bedhead hair, he was kind of beefy, and his beard looked like it had a bit of fried egg caught in it or something. Gross.

"My name's Sarah, Sarah Lockwood."

He just stood there, squinting at me. I felt like I'd intruded on him but it's not like he was composing a symphony or anything, he was just chopping wood.

"Sarah!" I heard a voice call.

Cathy. We both turned and watched as she made her way towards us looking so nice in another long flowing skirt, this time with a tunic of thin material over top. She was slightly out of breath as she came up to us, as if she'd been hurrying to reach us, and I was glad she did because it was pretty awkward standing there in front of this man who was my employer and who still hadn't said a word to me.

"Cliff, this is Sarah. She's going to be looking after the little ones."

Now, my parents have trained me so well that whenever I'm introduced to an adult I have this strong urge to hold out my hand and my hand had started to lift towards him but somehow the way he just stood there squinting made me think twice and I shoved my hands in my shorts pockets instead.

"Sarah's from the Maritimes," Cathy said.

His squint seemed to loosen up a bit.

"Woodstock, New Brunswick," Cathy added.

Immediately the squint tightened up again.

"Mainlander."

He bent to pick up another log and before he'd balanced it and split it in two Cathy had put her arm around my shoulder and led me back to the little ones, as she called them, who were still happily playing Ring Around A Rosie. You've got to love the way little kids can do the same thing over and over and over.

I told Cathy my plan—which was to do the t-shirt painting—and I said they could take the money off my pay since it was something I'd come up with without their knowledge, but she wouldn't hear of it and she thought it was a great idea and gave me a bunch of money from petty cash. She said that the man who owned the store was an old friend of theirs and would just charge any extra to their credit card.

So off we went. Rough Cove is about a half mile off the Cabot Trail so the road we walked on wasn't busy. We made our way in a kind of hand-holding elephant train to René's Wear House. The littlest one of the bunch was holding my (lead elephant's) hand and I pride myself on being able to understand kid talk.

"I gawp a haw," she said.

"Yes, yes," I said. "We're going up a hill!"

When I told René what we were there for he liked the idea so much he donated the little white cotton shirts and just charged for the fabric crayons and glitter, which meant that not only did I not have to charge anything, there was actually change.

Back at CC Lodge I saw Cliff fixing one of the big picnic tables and Cathy was talking to him so I went right up to them.

"Why, it's Sarah Sarah Lockwood from Woodstock," Cliff said to Cathy.

Okay, he was mocking me, but he seemed so much more friendly than he'd been earlier that I started to gab a bit.

"René was great," I said, reaching into my pocket for the money. "He was so nice with the little ones and he gave us the shirts for nothing—"

"And now every pint-sized tourist will want one," Cliff muttered, cutting me off.

He hammered a nail into the table before finishing his thought.

"Doubtless he ordered a truckload the moment you left. Perhaps he'll receive an honour from the Tourism Industry Association of Nova Scotia."

I was torn between thinking he sounded awfully jaded and being pleased that he'd spoken to me. He wasn't finished.

"René Leblanc's grandfather was a stonemason, fisherman, and seaman. His father, Henri, built his own dory at the age of fourteen and can still drink me under the table."

"Cliff," Cathy said.

She said it gently. It didn't seem so much like she was trying to stop him from giving me a bad impression as she was trying to soothe him.

"And René?" he continued, looking at Cathy and wincing when he said the name. "He joins the potters and the weavers that pander to the crowd that swells this place each summer." Say what you will, the man could talk.

"Plastic nonsense—"

Through all this he had been slowly working on

the picnic table, his meaty hand driving in a three-inch nail with just a few whacks. By "this place," I wasn't sure whether he meant CC Lodge or all of Cape Breton.

"We all need to make a living, Cliff," Cathy said.

She didn't seem mad at him even though he was being so surly.

"Oh yes, Miss Earnshaw, indeed we do."

"Actually, Sarah," Cathy said, still looking at him. "This isn't really my husband, it's an actor we hire to play a crusty Cape Bretoner for the tourists. The real Cliff is a computer nerd we keep in the attic."

Cliff's eyes flashed and his very white teeth showed in a grin beneath his black moustache.

"Ha!" he said.

Wham! went the hammer and I handed over the change and very happily went back to work.

SEVEN

THE KIDS LOVED THEIR shirts so much that they wore them all day every day over their bathing suits or shorts and by the end of the week they had popsicle drippings and what have you all down the front but it was fun. The only thing everyone had in common was that I printed each kid's name on his or her shirt, and that was good because then everyone in the resort could call them by their names and they liked that.

Now, the way it worked at CC Lodge, the little kids weren't stuck in daycare the whole day—nine to two were the hours—so part of my job was to help out with the more organized activities of the older kids from two to five. That wasn't as much fun for me, but it was absolutely low pressure since I was just a helper. So the kids at the lodge were taken care of the way kids usually are, and what was really weird was seeing how the adults spent their week. The men alternated between swimming, boating, and fishing and the women—it didn't matter whether they were full time mums or doctors and lawyers—ate.

Even though one of the breakfast choices was fruit and yogurt and muesli, the women always did grease—fried eggs, sausage, home fries—and coffee. Breakfast was prepared and served by live-in staff, then around eleven in the morning a woman named Joanne turned up with baskets of her amazing muffins. These were the sort of thing people would grab, with another cup of coffee, then continue with their activities or just plant themselves in a chair with a magazine. The staff, me included, lived on those muffins. Arvi arrived soon after that to oversee lunch. The form never varied, only the content, so there was always soup (sometimes cold, sometimes hot, always spicy), a big salad, and various wraps or pitas that seemed to follow a two-to-one vegetarian to carnivore rule. That meant that if there were three pitas two of them would be all veg and a third might have chicken or seafood in it. And dinner—well, like Cathy said, dinner was out of this world. It was the focal point of every mum's day.

I made this observation—that the women ate all the time and the men did sports—to Cathy at one of the bonfires and she laughed.

"You're absolutely right," she said. "The whole food thing evolved" (that was one of her favourite words, "evolved") "from a situation where I tried to be very minimal about food—everything was buffet style in the beginning—to the way it is now. Men love buffets, but the women seem to like to have their food brought to the table. That means more staff, of course, which makes the whole week more expensive." There was a pause and then she said, "But people do seem to keep coming."

Personally, I think it's way too expensive, but what do I know? Here are some of the comments from the guest book:

"Heaven." Jesse and Liam from Hantsport.

"A real retreat—thanks!" Brendan from Black Rock.

"After a 2-day TV/DVD withdrawal I was okay and even started looking forward to the hokey bingo game." Angela from Ottawa.

"The water pressure in the showers could be better." Sandy from Boston.

"I disagree. We come here to rough it a little. Everything's perfect." Risa from Wolfville.

"We'll be back." Michaela and Matt from Halifax.

Actually, Sandy from Boston had a point...the water pressure wasn't the best.

Thanks to that job I got to practice a lot of stuff in real life instead of just in my mind. For instance, I pretended to be a lot more outgoing than I really am.

"Hi, how are things? Can I get you anything? Where are you folks from?"

And the great part about it was that the guests would leave after a week and I could start fresh with a whole new set of people.

"Where are you folks from? Bingo starts at seven. Enjoy your stay!"

You know how when you go into a restaurant and you maybe feel all nervous about what to order and whether or not you should ask for this and that and you're wondering what the waiter thinks about you? Well, I don't worry about it anymore because I know from working at CC Lodge that the waiter has more on his mind than me. If he's grumpy he's probably grumpy with the cook or the hostess or the fact that some other waiter has taken the carafe of decaf coffee he just made and now he has to make another one. Or the ketchup bottles are empty, or the butter pats are frozen. Stuff like that. I mean, there's so much going on behind the scenes that the customers don't really impinge that much.

Cathy was the first adult I'd met since my grade one teacher that I wanted to be like. It was the summer I really became aware that there was no avoiding the fact that sooner or later everyone has to turn into a grownup and, I love my parents, but I didn't want to be like them. No way. But Cathy was the least annoying grownup I've ever met. She didn't even annoy Cliff and he was annoyed by everyone.

"Annoyed" is putting it mildly. It was actually kind of funny watching the vacation dads trying to hang around Cliff when he was building something or fishing or even just stacking firewood. He'd ignore them and ignore them and then finally growl at them. Most days he didn't even put in an appearance. You wouldn't call him the easiest guy to get along with, but Cathy was always nice to him. Even when something had gone wrong or she hadn't slept much because she'd been dashing around trying to make everything right for everybody, she didn't snap at him. She was the only one I ever saw make him laugh.

And she was just amazing with Cate. My mum was always after me whenever we'd had a fight to get things back to normal again as soon as possible, but no matter how much Cate snapped at her, Cathy pretty much left her alone.

Come to think of it, everyone pretty much left Cate alone.

EIGHT

YOU'D THINK THAT FOUR teenaged girls in a cabin on their own would have a pretty great time, wouldn't you? That first week I mostly fell asleep as soon as my head hit the pillow—I was so tired from learning on the job, pitching in, and having to be friendly all the time—but by the second week I was lying awake in the top bunk listening to peals of laughter coming from the BHB girls and wishing I'd been randomly assigned to their cabin.

Tara was nice. She always asked after the little kids and seemed to enjoy hearing about them so I always asked how it was in the lodge and she always said the same thing.

"Not too bad."

Then we'd gather up our toothbrushes and stuff and head out to the porta-potty—it was the kind that had a mirror and a little sink in it—and by the time we got back to our cabin Cate had usually come in and settled on her bunk and was giving off Do No Disturb vibrations. I guess she washed and flossed in her house because I never saw her line up for a porta-potty or take a shower at the lodge.

"Maybe she's, you know, like *him* and washes at the pump."

By "him" we knew Ellen was referring to Cliff.

"Yeah, I'm, like, out there at, like, dawn, on the way to set up for breakfast and he's hunched over the pump, slappin' at himself with cold water."

This was one of those comments that made me realize a) how great my hours were that I didn't have to get up so early and b) Ellen was way more clued in to what went on behind the scenes than I was. It turned out that Tara had seen him too.

"Mm. I think those are the nights he hasn't slept at all," she said.

You could tell by the way she looked when we wanted more info that she already felt bad about gossiping. But we insisted she elaborate on this.

"Well, I've seen him up there."

She pointed to the small window that was on our side of the cabin. If you looked out of it in the daytime, you saw a perfectly pleasant wooded mountain, but at night, which it was when we were having this conversation, it looked wild.

"They say the plateau is covered with bogs and that the lakes turn black with peat. Kind of like tundra. And because of the constant winds blowing up there the trees are all stunted and gnarly."

This was the kind of thing Tara would know. She was one of those kids who could tell you exactly how big the hole in the ozone layer was over the Antarctic and how many trees it took to make the Saturday edition of the newspaper. Stuff like that. Fortunately Ellen broke in.

"Creepy," she said.

"Mm," said Tara. "You think so?"

"Duh. He's got a wife workin' her buns off and he goes *mountain* climbing?"

"He works hard too," Tara said.

She looked over her shoulder when she said it as though she expected someone might overhear us. It was true that when he was around, Cliff worked hard. I mean, he could fix anything.

"And there's the thing he does with the lobsters."

"Yeah, what *is* that?" Ellen said. "I go into the kitchen the other night and he's, like, *fondling* them."

Tara saw the look on my face and said it wasn't what it sounded like.

"He was calming them," she said.

Apparently, on lobster night, Cliff had come into the kitchen and taken each lobster and held it upside down, with the pincers and head on the counter, then slowly moved his fingers upward along each of their backs and over the curves of their tails.

"He hypnotized them," Ellen said. "They've got these rubber bands on their fingers, they're about to be boiled alive, they should be fighting like crazy, right? And instead their little crustacean bums are in the air and they're blissed out."

"They just stayed like that," Tara said. "No struggling."

"I mean, if the guy can hypnotize *lobsters*, maybe he can hypnotize *us*. Maybe he's hypnotized Cathy—"

Neither Tara nor I said anything, but I know I was wondering why else a nice person like Cathy would put up with such a grump.

"If he weren't so hot—" Ellen said.

"Mm," Tara agreed and, once again, I began to feel unmistakably out of place as a) I found him gross and b) it didn't feel right to talk about someone's dad that way.

The someone whose dad he was walked in just then and by the way we all went silent I guess she thought we were talking about her. It was deadly quiet in our cabin so we could hear the BHB girls laughing and someone playing a guitar. Todd from Maine played guitar. Did that mean there was a party with boys going on and we were all just sitting quietly in our cabin?

"Well, I'm outta here," Ellen said. "Anyone coming with me?"

Tara and I were already in our pyjamas with our teeth brushed, though I sure wanted to go and I'll bet she did too.

"No thanks," Cate said in one of her typical two-word sentences.

She threw herself down on her bunk below Tara's and lay there face up with her eyes open. Ellen's eyebrows were raised in invitation but it seemed so unfriendly to just leave Cate like that, especially after going all quiet when she'd come in, that neither Tara nor I could make a move to go partying. Would we have hesitated at all if she hadn't been our employers' daughter? I don't think so.

"I need a hostess gift," Ellen said, and there was a sound from Cate like a disgusted snort.

Tara seemed to feel sorry for Cate and I sort of did too, but I felt sorrier for me because I was about to miss out on a party. A real party with just us kids instead of a bonfire night where we talked about the destruction of habitat and the horrors of genetic engineering. I reached under my bunk and handed Ellen my first care package. She rummaged around, rejected the mint-flavoured waxed dental floss, and took the chocolate-covered almonds.

"Are these Fair Trade?" she asked.

I glanced at Cate, who didn't blink or snort, then at Tara, who rolled her eyes, then I just shook my head at Ellen.

"Tsk, tsk," she said, waving her finger at me but giving me a big grin.

Then the door closed and she was gone. As Tara started to climb into her bunk she made an attempt at conversation.

"Didn't you help at the Bingo game tonight, Cate?"

"I did."

"How did you like that?"

"Not much."

It was hard work, and if it had been me I'd have given up, but Tara kept trying.

"It must be strange having all these people vacationing around what is actually your home."

I was expecting her to say, "It is," but there was no comment at all.

"And then, if you and your mum and dad ever want to get away I guess you have to take your holidays in the fall or winter."

Still no comment.

"On the other hand it's so beautiful here…" Tara's sentence just petered out.

Maybe I should have tried to help with the conversation, but I just lay on my bunk feeling awful. Cate wasn't talking, Tara had stopped talking, and I wasn't at the party. The laughter and singing from the BHB cabin was torturing me—why couldn't my mum have put ear plugs in my care package? I tried counting back from two hundred, which usually puts me to sleep, but I got through the count twice and I was still wide awake. I must have finally drifted off to sleep, though, because suddenly the bed was shaking and Ellen was climbing into the top bunk. I couldn't resist letting her know she'd woken me up.

"How was the party?" I whispered.

"You didn't miss a thing," she whispered back.

"Really?"

She hung her head over the edge of her bed and looked at me upside down.

"I'm being *nice*, Sarah. It was awesome…you know Jason? He goes—"

She was interrupted by one of those familiar two-word utterances.

"Shut. Up."

Still hanging upside down, Ellen held out her hands and mimed choking Cate. Then she loudly swung her upper body back into bed and loudly settled herself in for the night. I was wondering if she'd keep loudly tossing and turning, but I guess the partying had tired her out because before long I heard seriously sleepy breathing from overhead. I wanted to get up and look out the window to see if Cliff was out there, but I was afraid to make any noise because Cate was such a grump. Was he up there on the mountain top? Even in summer it was cold at night, and I imagined that up there it would be pretty brutal. Maybe there'd be one of those thick clouds pressing down.

Creepy.

I just had to get some sleep myself so, again, I started counting. Two hundred, one ninety-nine... one ninety-eight...one ninety-...

NINE

WHENEVER I MOAN about how nothing ever happens in Woodstock, my dad, predictably, quotes a supposedly ancient Chinese curse: "May you live in interesting times."

The first couple of weeks at CC Lodge should have been interesting enough. It easily took that long for us high school kids to get the hang of our jobs and being away from home. Living away from home was the hardest. In Cape Breton there was no dad to drive me anywhere I felt like going and no mum to tell every minute detail of my irritations to. Writing letters just didn't fill in that gap because a) by the time I'd written a letter and gotten one back so much would have happened in between, and b) I was too busy and too tired to write anyway.

Tara and I did manage to boldly go to one of the BHB parties, at least, but it went on till five in the morning, which means she got one hour of sleep and I got two. The next day I felt energized and fabulous and I was so pleased with myself, playing with the little kids and being friendly with the parents, "Hi, my name's Sarah, where you folks from?" Then—wham—the day after that I was exhausted.

"It's not the sleep you get the night before the marathon that matters," my dad would say whenever I'd been stressing about a test or something, "it's two nights before that's important."

Man, do I ever understand that now. The first day after our party marathon I'd felt more energetic than usual, but for the second one I could hardly keep my eyes open. The poor little munchkins didn't know what had happened to their Sarah. I tried lying down on the floor and letting them crawl all over me, but it turns out that only works with one kid at a time. They hurt.

Ellen was clearly pleased that Tara and I had stayed up all night with her, even if we did wimp out the next time. It was soon after that, about the third week in July, that Ellen and I really bonded. It was at another bonfire night, quite late, and the sky over the water was the most amazing purple colour—I can't describe it. Behind us were the black mountains and in front of us was the ocean and that purple sky and no street lights. It was beautiful and eerie at the same time.

"Where's Cate?" Cathy asked.

"She's in the dining hall," said Jason.

"No, she's taking a shower," said Hilary.

"Actually, she's in our cabin," said Tara who had just arrived herself and so presumably was the last one to see her.

"Oh, for heaven's sake," Cathy said and she pressed her lips together, which was the only way you could tell she was really mad. "Tara would you—? Never mind, I'll go myself."

Cathy strode off to fetch Cate. There was a long silence during which I know I was wondering whether Cathy would be able to get Cate to come join us. I guess I wasn't the only one because the silence was finally broken by Ellen holding her hand to her mouth and making a "ch, ch" sound like a policeman's crackly radio message to headquarters.

"Uh, ch, ch, we have a situation, here…uh, ch, ch, officer heading into potentially dangerous territory…requesting back up, do you copy?"

That broke everyone up and Jason from Ontario jumped right in.

"Roger, we copy, ch, ch, is the suspect armed? Over."

If it had been just us high school students there I know the joke could have gone on a lot longer but Marsha took over the adult role in Cathy's absence.

"Okay, okay, everyone."

She didn't even have to say anything like "Let's not have a laugh at Cate's expense," or "Show some respect," or anything like that, just "Okay, okay, everyone," and we all went quiet again.

But it was a different quiet now, because each of us knew he or she wasn't the only one who found Cate a little weird. And in that quiet we heard the crunch of two pairs of feet on the beach and sure enough Cathy and Cate took their places around the bonfire.

"Hi, Cate," Tara said.

Cate actually looked at her and said hi back.

Well, that was a breakthrough.

Since we were all settled into our jobs and cabins there was no need for games anymore and people just started talking, occasionally singing, and it was pretty fun being out there at night under the stars. For once the conversation wasn't only about the lodge or world news and the bonfire talk turned to what Cathy called "popular culture." A rumour was circulating (one of the guests had started it) that Tom Hanks owned an island nearby.

"So where is Tom Hanks' island?" Hilary asked.

"He hasn't bought it, yet," said Brittany. "He's just looking."

You could see the island they were talking about from the shore. It was the only island out there and that was its name, Only Island.

"Do you think he's friends with Uma Thurman?" one of the BHB girls asked.

Apparently Uma Thurman had bought a whole island somewhere in Nova Scotia when she was married to Ethan Hawke.

"You guys talking about Only Island?" said Jason. "I know who owns it."

Everyone turned to look at him.

"My sister told me when she heard I got this job. It's not Tom Hanks, it's the soap guy, what's-his-name. You know, Ellis Bell."

When I think back, I can see the reaction on each of the fire-reddened faces. Most of them were disappointed, I was excited, and Cathy and Ellen actually stiffened a little.

"Who's Ellis Bell?" asked Tara.

Before I could say anything (and risk a week of jokes worse than dental floss) Ellen answered.

"My last boss," she said. "That's who."

Whoa.

Everyone was surprised by this news, including Cathy, who was looking at Ellen with her mouth open. It didn't strike me as odd, but when I thought about it later, I realized that Cathy should have known who Ellen's last employer was, shouldn't she? That would have been the first thing on her resume, wouldn't it? I was so caught up and excited by the announcement myself that Cathy's surprise didn't register as unusual.

"You mean I've been sharing a bunk with

someone who's met Ellis Bell and I didn't even know it?" I said.

"Who's Ellis Bell?" Tara asked again.

"He's the star of *Willow Heights.*"

"The soap opera?"

"Yes!"

Everyone who had just looked disappointed before looked disgusted now, and I did a cowardly thing.

"My mum just loves him," I said.

"You can tell your mum he's, like, totally weird," Ellen said.

Ellen was clearly prepared to tell us all sorts of juicy gossip then and there but she never got the chance.

"Do we have to listen to anything about these shallow people?" Cate said.

It was the longest sentence she'd ever spoken to either of us.

"We don't have TV, so…" Cathy said.

She and Cate may have been having mother–daughter issues, but they sure agreed about the worthlessness of popular culture.

There was some trashing of TV stars and movie stars and then the conversation petered out and I felt like Ellen and I were the only ones interested in talking about something other than the environment and world peace.

There I was, dying to hear more about my heartthrob, but Ellen didn't know that because I'd deflected it onto my mum, so I wanted to find a way to let her know I'd be interested in hearing her stories even if Cate and Tara weren't. Actually, Tara might have been—she wasn't stuck up, just smart—but it turned out that I didn't have to find a way, a way presented itself: I got sick.

And the times got way more interesting.

TEN

"THE BODY HAS ITS OWN WISDOM."

Another of my dad's quotes. Usually it's his way of telling me that he thinks my headache or twisty stomach is because I don't want to go to: school...the grandparents'...the dentist...(fill in the blank). I never thought there was anything to it, but I certainly wonder about it when I look back on my summer sickness.

Oh, what a whopper of a cold I had. I know what you're thinking. Everyone who works around kids gets colds, right? But I know all that, and I know that when you're around munchkins a lot you should wash your hands all the time, carry one of those little travel-sized waterless hand sanitizer thingies in case you can't wash your hands (my mum sent one in the care package), not put your hands to your nose and eyes, blah blah blah. I ignored all this. I even, and this is what makes me most suspicious now, neglected to take zinc lozenges the second I knew a cold was coming. I always know a cold's coming by the slightest little scratchiness in my throat and if I pop a zinc right away I can actually avoid it entirely. If I pop them throughout the cold it can be over in about two days.

I didn't do any of those things.

I felt the scratchiness early in the morning. By the time two o'clock rolled around I had a really sore throat and I was occasionally seized with fits of sneezing. I wasn't hungry at dinnertime, and dinner was always so good at CC Lodge, and I skipped the bonfire to go straight to bed.

When Tara and Ellen and Cate came in later that night I hadn't really slept, just lain there feeling sorry for myself. I was dying for some chat but they were all exhausted and so they just flopped on their bunks and conked out. I didn't think I could sleep and then the next thing I knew I was waking myself with one of those awful snorty sounds you make when you can't really breathe or you're overtired. It was a restless night of feeling like I wasn't getting any sleep at all, and feeling mad about that, then waking myself up again with a snort. On and on.

Unfortunately I wasn't the only one woken up by my snorty sounds. Even Tara stopped trying to protect my feelings after awhile and stuffed her head under her pillow. Ellen had already done that. Though I was underneath her bunk and couldn't see, I'd heard her groan, roll over heavily, and pack the pillow around her ears. It was a pretty rough night.

"Delightful company," Cate said as she left the cabin the next morning.

I kept my eyes shut and listened to the sounds of zippers being zipped and feet being shoved into shoes.

"I'll tell Cathy she can't work today," Tara said. "Will you write a note for when she wakes up?"

"Sure," Ellen said.

Tara left and when Ellen finished dressing I heard the scritch-scratch of a pen on paper. When the door shut after her I opened my eyes and read the note she'd left beside my head: *Go back to sleep, Snothead, we'll cover for ya.*

I did go back to sleep and when I woke up the next time it was to the sound of knocking on the cabin door. When I tried to say "Come in," my throat really hurt and it wasn't loud enough so whoever it was didn't hear me. There was a rustling sound outside and the next thing I knew Arvi's face appeared at the little window on my side—the one that gave Tara her glimpse of Cliff wandering at night—and I made a motion with my hand for her to come in. There were rustling sounds again as she retraced her steps and came in the door.

"Poor Sarah," she said in her singsong voice. "To have a cold in summer is not fun at all, not at all."

Then she moved my sandals to where I could slide into them easily and somehow I was on my feet with my sleeping bag wrapped around me and Arvi was leading me along the little footpath that forked away from the staff cabins. She was carrying my pillow and an extra blanket.

I was too stupefied to register what was going on and just shuffled along behind Arvi. I knew if we stayed on the path we'd eventually emerge at the back of the office and I suppose I thought that was where we were really headed. Just when I felt I'd better stop and take a break or my head would explode, Arvi did stop. Right in front of the ice house. Part of my fuzzy brain had known she was taking me to the ice house, but the last time I'd looked in there it had been filled with old oars and buoys and a chair with a broken back.

She opened the door. The stuff that they stored in there had been taken away and all that was in its place was a cot that reached end to end. It reminded me of a book my dad had at home that was filled with pictures of unusual building projects and one of them was a meditation hut that was actually a renovated outhouse. If this had been an outhouse it would have been a three- or even four-holer, but it still seemed awfully small compared to our cabin.

Arvi was fussing and muttering. My head was all woozy from the walk and I just wanted to lie down.

Even though she hadn't yet told me that this was where I was going to stay, Arvi spread my sleeping bag out on the cot and I crept into it gratefully. Snuggling into that bag on the cot when I was so achy and sick was delicious. I didn't even thank Arvi, I just gave her a little wave and rolled over on to my side. Right there, level with my pillow, were these characters carved into the wall: I♥C.

"We'll check on you," I heard Arvi say.

Then the door shut and I was in blackness. Almost before that fact could register I heard Arvi stop outside and wait as someone approached. Cathy.

"Ah, Missus—"

Arvi called Cliff and Cathy "Mister and Missus," even though everyone, including the little kids, called them by their first names.

"Is she settled already?"

"Yes, yes, but Mister was, I think, not pleased—"

Tired as I was I wanted to stay awake and hear any tidbits about "Mister."

"Oh, Arvi, did Cliff give you a hard time?"

There was no sound so I gathered Arvi was nodding her head.

"Yes, he has odd notions about the ice house… we used to play in it as kids…he didn't want it moved here…tell him—no, I'll tell him—it was Cate's idea."

They chuckled, the way my mum and I do when we've figured out how to steer my dad in the direction we want him to go. But Cliff didn't strike me as the kind of guy you did that with. He struck me as the kind of guy you left alone. Or else.

Why did they put me here if it was such a sentimental spot for them?

Cate.

Tell him—no, I'll tell him—it was Cate's idea.

Cate had complained that I'd kept the three of them awake all night.

Delightful company.

So this was Cate's doing. If I'd been feeling well I'd have loved it—I could have pretended I was a hermit living just on the edge of civilization and sneaking into town like a black bear to forage—but as it was I just felt lonely. Occasionally I'd hear the distant healthy-happy sounds of a vacationer taking out a kayak, or of laughter, or of doors slamming, and that made me feel even lonelier.

Now Cliff would have one more gripe against Sarah Sarah Lockwood.

Mister was, I think, not pleased.

These notions lodged in my poor heavy head—delightful company, not pleased, I♥C—but I was too sick and tired to really care.

ELEVEN

HAVE YOU EVER FALLEN asleep, or thought you were asleep, then woken up, or thought you were awake, and you couldn't move? It's terrifying. It's like your arms and legs and lips and eyelids won't do anything your brain wants them to and yet you're sure you're awake. That's what was happening to me. I couldn't tell if I'd been asleep a long time and I was just waking up or if only seconds had passed since Arvi had left me and I'd almost fallen asleep and now was caught in this awful paralyzed state.

"Move!" I told my arms.

Nothing.

"Open!" I screamed at my eyes.

They stayed shut. And as much as I was trying to scream at my arms and legs and eyelids, my mouth stayed shut too. None of my body parts were working.

Except my ears. I could hear the wind, and something else. Movement. Outside the cabin.

Then the realization hit me that I wasn't in the cabin, I was in the ice house, all alone, and struggling to move, and the sound when I heard it the next time instantly brought the picture into my mind of a black bear snuffling around, his black nose sniffing around the base of the ice house, his black claws exploring the shingles—

With one massive effort I flung out my arms and legs and kicked off the sleeping bag and gulped in a big breath of air and pounded on the wall and screamed at the top of my lungs.

"Help! Help!"

At least, that's what I thought I'd done. It felt like I'd thrown myself into a huge convulsion to shake myself out of that awful paralysis when, in fact, I was just lying there inside the sleeping bag.

I was fully awake, though, and what a relief that was. The only hint I had that some time had passed since Arvi had left me was that I was lying on my back and not on my side. I distinctly recalled being on my side at first and seeing I♥C. Now there I was flat on my back with both arms inside the sleeping bag and folded across my stomach. There was no evidence of thrashing and no sound that could be taken for a bear snuffling around outside either.

Even though I could still feel the adrenaline throughout my arms and legs, it was such a relief to realize I'd just been caught in one of those half-awake half-asleep states. The sound of the snuffling bear was probably just my own plugged up nose trying to breathe and in that in-between state it had sounded different to my ears. As I lay there adjusting to this feeling of not being paralyzed and not being mauled by a bear I could tell by the distant sounds that it was probably early evening and I had in fact slept for quite a while. Once my eyes adjusted I could even tell that it wasn't exactly pitch black in the ice house, either. There was light coming in through a few cracks in the walls and around the door.

My awareness of my cold symptoms had been driven away first by terror and then the release from terror, but now, unfortunately, I was sufficiently my self again to be aware of the achiness of my body and the stuffiness in my head. My dad says our heads weigh sixteen to eighteen pounds and normally I don't feel my head at all, but once the distractions were over I sure did. I sank back into my pillow and rested. My eyes couldn't have been closed for two minutes when I♥C appeared against the dark. It was like when you look at something—a lamp, say—then look at the wall and a shadowy image of the lamp appears against the wall. And it moves. You can't make the silhouette stay still. It slides diagonally down the wall until you bring it back up high again with your eyes and then it starts its diagonal slide again. Only in this case, the wall was my closed eyelids and the shadowy letters were, in fact, greyish white against the blackness. A ghostly I♥C floated diagonally across my vision in the darkness, disappeared, and then reappeared again only to drift diagonally down.

That's not exactly scary except that, in the case of the lampshade, you see the shadow ghost because you've just been looking at the lampshade and then you've looked away. It had been hours since I'd seen the carving on the wall—how could its ghost shadow be floating in front of me now?

It must have been the effects of being sick, away from home, and banished from the cozy cabin. What else could be making me have such a terrible night? Even as a little kid I don't think I ever had a night like that one, and I'd had a bad fever when I was four with hallucinations and everything, but when I came out of those my mum or dad would be there urging me to suck on a popsicle or offering to read to me. That night had been harder on my parents than me. My mum still shivers whenever she thinks of it.

I started to dream. I thought it was morning and I was back in Woodstock and my dad had already headed out the door for his run and Mum and I were downstairs watching our week's worth of *Willow Heights*. Then a new idea came to me. No, I wasn't watching *Willow Heights*, I was in Willow Heights, the town, and if I went to the stand of willows I'd be sure to meet Ellis Bell.

Instantly I stood before the swaying willows. *Swish, swish* in front of me like a multi-layered curtain. Part of me tried to prolong the moment and part of me just wanted to get through the swaying curtain, because I knew who would be in there. I walked so slowly that it seemed to take ages to move through the leaves—the way a car moves slowly through the automatic car wash and those big thick strips of cloth swish back and forth over it—and at some point in my walk the willow leaves, though soft, almost seemed to be pushing me gently along, deeper and deeper.

There he was. He was facing away from me, which gave me time to compose myself, so that when he sensed I was there and turned towards me I would be ready to greet him as though it were perfectly normal for me to be there in Willow Heights and even right inside the willows at that moment. He did turn to me, looking so dreamy and handsome, but I wasn't ready for what he said.

"Where's Cate?"

The question so jarred me that I was suddenly sucked back through the willows at high speed.

This time, I remembered I was lying in the ice house and I heard the gusty wind and I heard my own breathing, too, and this time my panic didn't turn it into a snuffling bear. But it annoyed me so much that I actually moaned.

"Ohhh!"

Weirdly, outside, there was an answering moan.

"Ohhh!"

Could that be? Maybe I hadn't been as wide awake as I'd thought at first and had only dreamed I'd groaned and then, now that I really was awake, I'd made the second groan myself. I listened hard but there was quite a wind, a wind so strong that the branch of a tree rattled now and then against the roof of the ice house. Well, at least I was sufficiently awake and calm enough to realize it was the wind causing that particular noise. But—

"Ohhh!"

There it was again. Definitely not made by me this time and definitely closer sounding. Whoever was making this sound was coming closer and closer and I realized it wasn't a moan so much as a roar.

"Arrgghh!"

Light glimmered through the cracks and around the door. I tried to focus on those glimmers of light but the combination of the rattling of the limb on the roof and the footsteps coming nearer and the howling wind worked on my imagination. I knew just who would make an angry noise like that. And he wouldn't care who heard him and he wouldn't come tiptoeing, he'd come with stomps like the ones I heard now, stopping just outside.

Mister was, I think, not pleased.

The door to the ice house was flung open. I only realized I'd put my hands to my face in horror when I felt the icy cold of my fingers on my cheeks.

"Begone!"

Black against the rectangle of light from the night sky was the big beefy scary bearded figure of Cliff, roaring at me.

The next thing I remember I really had thrashed my way out of my sleeping bag. I was all twisted up and I'd knocked a box of tissues clear to the end of the cot.

Wait a minute, I thought as I bent over to retrieve them, *there were no tissues here*. Then I noticed that someone (Arvi? Cathy? Tara?) had obviously made a visit to the ice house and left me a few items: an overturned milk crate that held the tissues, a thermos of water (that had toppled over in my thrashing), a little wicker waste basket, and a tiny, battery-powered lamp that was hanging in the corner above my head. It gave a nice little bluish glow to the place that was dull enough to sleep by but light enough to make it way less scary. How long had those things been there?

I blew my nose, drank some water, and settled back down, figuring that all of the night's events must have been dreams, even though they had all seemed so real. My hands, when I put them to my face, weren't icy at all, but hot. There really was a heck of a wind out there and a branch really was banging on the roof occasionally, but now I thought it sounded kind of nice. Almost comforting. Still, there was the issue of the things that had appeared in the ice house. Someone really had come into the ice house and it must have been after dark because I was sure—pretty sure—that those things weren't there the first couple of times I'd woken up.

I sank back into my sleeping bag feeling a little silly. "Begone," for heaven's sake. No one says "begone," not even a grump like Cliff. He probably really was sentimental, just like Cathy said. *I♥C* probably stood for *I love Cathy* and he'd carved it when they were younger and didn't like the idea of her turning over their special place to some mainlander who couldn't appreciate it.

He was just private, that's all, a character, used to living alone most of the year with his wife and their only child. Not everybody is sociable. Not everybody likes to talk talk talk. Everybody's different. I made a mental note to myself that I really had to watch my imagination and then I closed my eyes and knew that this time I wouldn't have any more nightmares.

Still, after a night like that, part of me couldn't help being a little bit uneasy. I rolled over and fell asleep on my other side so that I was facing the door.

TWELVE

THE WORST PART of a cold is around the second day, when it's no longer coming on but has definitely arrived. I was so stuffed up that I was mouth breathing, which I hate. Just as you're dropping off to sleep you jerk awake and your mouth is all dry yet sticky so you try to generate a little saliva but that triggers the desire to swallow, which not only hurts your sore throat but cuts off your only way of breathing since your nasal passages are already blocked, so there's a mini explosion in your ears and you realize you haven't breathed in a while and you want to and so you open your mouth again to suck in air…and your mouth's all dry yet sticky and on it goes. I hate that.

It was at this stage in my cold that Ellen made her first foray to the ice house to visit me. She poked her head in and I was so happy to see her. Some people like to be left alone to curl into a ball when they're sick, but not me.

"Up for visitors?"

I nodded, my mouth hanging open.

"Ya look awful."

"I fee awfuh."

She had a pile of magazines that she'd brought for me.

"Stinks in here," she said.

"Thangs."

"Not *you*. The room. Stuffy."

She shoved the door wide open and left it like that. When I pushed myself up so I could sit I felt a crackle in my sinuses, but it just lasted a moment and they were immediately stuffed again.

Ellen had cleared off the milk box and was using it as a stool to perch on.

"At dozen look too comfable," I said.

"So I'll get waffle marks on my butt," she said.

Then she put one of the magazines between herself and the milk box.

"Better."

"Gud."

"Heard the news?"

I didn't even have time to answer before Ellen slapped her forehead.

"I wasn't supposed to tell!"

Now I was really curious.

"Okay, okay, don't tell I told, but Cate went missing *all* afternoon yesterday. I'm in the kitchen after lunch and Arvi goes, 'Where's Cate?' and Todd and I go, 'Dunno,' and Arvi's ticked 'cause right after lunch she likes to get prep for dinner started and that's Cate's job—you know, I've got this theory? I bet Cate gets to do dinner prep so she doesn't have to actually work with anybody. She can just be all alone dicing and slicing." Ellen mimed chopping vegetables. "Anyway, so Cathy pitches in and does prep—" now Ellen was chopping vegetables with her lips pressed together and I had to laugh "—and then it gets, like, *comical.* I mean every time someone walks by it's, 'Where's Cate? Where's Cate?' No one's seen her. A couple of people suggest in here, but *you're* in here, so she's—Gandhi, gone, outta here, nowhere to be found—then, around five-thirty maybe, who comes wandering up from the direction of the shore?"

"Wawa she doondown there?"

"Writing bad poetry, probably—who knows and who cares? Though actually, I preferred not having her around except for the extra work that—oops, that's what I *wasn't* supposed to do. Make you feel bad 'cause we're shorthanded. Sorry."

There was no time to feel guilty because just then the door slammed shut. Ellen and I looked at each other in the faint blue light.

"Wind," she said.

"'Cept there isn' any."

She leaped up and opened the door. I saw her look up and down the path and heard her check all around the ice house. Then she came back and propped the door open again, this time with a rock.

"You'll have to push harder next time," she said in a loud voice.

It reminded me of when Marsha had used a loud voice to let whoever had been in the ice house know that we were leaving. It had been Cate.

"You fink it wuz her?" I asked.

"Probably," Ellen said.

"Fink she heard?"

"I could care *less*. Serves her right for sneakin' around."

Several things went through my mind at once. At least if Cate had heard everything it wasn't me who'd said anything bad, I was just listening to Ellen. Also, it bugged me a little that Ellen said "could care less" when you're supposed to say "couldn't care less," but these were the least of my worries. My big worry was that Cate was mad that I was in her hideout—but if that was the case, why did she have them put me here?

Cliff! Cliff was the one who was always wandering around, maybe he'd been listening outside the door.

"Ewww," said Ellen. "That gives me the creeps."

It gave me the creeps too.

"Look," I said, pulling back my pillow and showing her the carved letters on the wall.

"Cathy must've done it," she said. "When they were young. *I love Cliff.*"

"Mebbe it wuz him," I said.

"I love Cathy? Naw. Even *nice* guys don't do little hearts." Then she thought of something. "Hey, there are so many Cs around here, maybe it's *I love Cate.*"

I was actually about to say that the letters looked too old to be about Cate when it became clear that Ellen wasn't serious.

"But who would write *that?*" she said, quite loudly and I felt that even if it wasn't Cate out there I wouldn't want anyone else to hear either. "Maybe she did it herself!"

Torn between finding this funny and worrying that someone could hear us, I motioned for Ellen to stop by drawing my hand across my throat.

Then she did a wonderful thing. She straightened my cot and fluffed my pillows and picked up all the tissues that had missed the basket, and piled the magazines so that the covers all faced up and the spines were aligned. Have you noticed that when you're sick you can't take even the kind of mess that normally seems just right?

"You'd mega guh nurse."

"That's what Ellis said, too."

My whole body, muffled as it was by snot and pyjamas, perked up at that name.

THIRTEEN

WE'RE ALL SO FULL of ourselves! Here I was, feeling isolated and rotten in the ice house, cut off from all the little daily chat and gossip that goes on at the lodge, thinking, "If only I can not seem too sick and smelly she'll stay and talk to me," when she was dying to tell her stories.

"I was, like, *so* excited. My first real job. Even if it was just for summer."

"Ad fer Ellis Bell!" I interrupted.

"Well, they gave me her name—Isobel—but—"

"Thass her nabe? 'Isobel Bell.' Thass stupid."

"Well, his real name's Edgar Linton—"

I knew that.

"Is she ad actor?"

"Rich bitch."

"Ah."

Just like Arabella Guring!

"Where was I?"

"'Cited."

"Right. I mean I knew they were rich because not only were they paying for my flight down and all that, but I was expected to be on duty from seven in the morning till seven at night."

"Wow."

"I know, huh?"

I thought of my own hours with the munchkins at the lodge and how even though I loved it, by two in the afternoon it was hard not to look at the clock every few minutes to see when the mums and dads would be coming. She had them for twice that long.

"They should do a study. The Effect of Serial Nannies on Young Children."

Cereal nannies?

"People like them go through nannies like candy."

I didn't much care to hear my heartthrob being referred to as "people like them," but I was used to keeping my crush on Ellis to myself. Anyway, she was probably really referring to Arabella. I mean, Isobel.

"House looked normal enough from outside. White. Dormers. Coupla bay windows. Only when you saw it from the back you'd go, 'Oh, it's like, *grand.*' The front was, like, set into this knobby hill so it looked like two storeys? But from the back you saw four."

"Wow."

"So I ring the doorbell and wait and my first thought is, like, if this were a movie Edgar Linton would fall madly in love with me at first sight—"

I didn't interrupt with, "Oh, Ellen," or anything because I know that if it had been me in her place I'd have had exactly the same thought. As soon as she heard she'd gotten the job she did her research.

"Bought one of those rags—"

"*Soapworl* or *Daydime Drama?*"

"*Soapworld.*"

"Uh-huh."

"And there he was and…those hafta be contact lenses, huh? No one's eyes are that intense green, right?"

"Codtacs?"

"Nope. His eyes are that green."

"Fought so."

"You know, Cathy would go, 'toxicity.'"

"Wha?"

"She's into iridology. You know, they, like, look in your eye and say you should take milk thistle for your liver and stop drinking hot chocolate, stuff like that. Does it for people here if they want."

"Rilly?"

"Yeah, and she says there's no such thing as genuinely green eyes."

"Bud…"

At least Ellen and I were in the clear for toxicity as far as Cathy was concerned. My eyes are blue and hers are brown.

"I know, like, who cares? They're so gorgeous."

"Zackly."

"Just thought I'd mention it. Anyways, there I am thinking the green-eyed god would be standing there falling in love at first sight with me, but it was the errand lady."

"Erran?"

"Yeah. She turned out to be very nice and full of neat stories about the brats—"

"Ellen..."

"Oh, lighten up."

"Whass an erran lady?"

"Say you're really rich and really busy. You hire this lady to be, like, a homemaker, only she doesn't clean or cook or any of that, she does the *thinking* about it. So say we're going away for the weekend? She'd decide what everyone—*everyone*—Edgar, Isobel, the children—would take and she'd lay it out, or maybe just make a list that could be ticked off as things were packed away."

"Jeepers."

"Think about it, I mean, there are actually stats on how much time you spend at, like, stoplights and stuff over your lifetime. Did you know you spend maybe three months opening junk mail or something? So this chicky—her name was Marie— handles all that and no time is wasted."

When I thought about it, it kind of made

sense. The number of times I've gotten dressed for school in the morning then changed my mind and completely undressed and re-dressed again is ridiculous. I even have a recurring dream about it—a frustration dream, my dad calls it—where my mum is calling out, "It's 8:15, Sarah!" and I'm in front of my mirror wearing yellow tights, plaid skirt and yellow sweater and I think "yuck" and strip it all off and look for something else and my mum's saying "8:20," and now I'm in green tights, black skirt, green sweater and no matter what I do I keep coming up with these stupid matched outfits and my mum's calling and calling…so I guess a Marie would save me some agony.

But what if I didn't like what she chose for me?

"That's her job, though, to know, you know?"

"Bud whad if she dozen?"

"Fire 'n hire, but that's her job, so she *does* know."

I decided I'd better keep quiet and listen for a while or maybe Ellen would get fed up with me. And I really needed to make a trip to the porta-potty, but I didn't want to interrupt her anymore than I already had. I just looked at her through my sticky eyes.

"Poor baby. I should go, huh? You wanna sleep?"

I shook my head. "Sday," I said.

She stayed. It didn't take much.

"Marie takes me into the kitchen and apologizes 'cause she can't make me a cup of tea even, because no cooking is actually ever done there. When she sees my expression she, like, *titters.*"

"'I know,'" she says, "'but the Lintons have all their meals delivered by Boxed Bounty to the set or whatever spa they're at, so I thought it would be simpler—and more economical—to order for the children, too, and not hire a full-time cook. Parties are catered, of course.'"

"I look around at this kitchen that's just *begging* for someone to whip something up in it—there's, like, a gas stove with six burners, a stand-up freezer to match the fridge, two microwave ovens—I'm thinking, why?—and a built-in wall oven, the counter tops are real marble—and I go over and open the fridge. Nothing. Nada. I mean, our fridge at home gets empty but it's always, like, onion skins on the bottom shelf, fuzzy gunge. This sucker *glistened.*"

"'I can have that stocked for you, if you like,' Marie says, 'but Boxed Bounty will do anything... vegan, macrobiotic...all you teenage girls are vegetarians, right?'"

"Now, personally, I'd been thinking in my heart of hearts maybe I am? Who wants to eat tortured critters? But I don't like being lumped in, you know? I should have gone, 'Actually, I'll have a bacon cheeseburger with fries,' but instead I go, 'Okay.' When in Rome and all that. It's only two months, right?"

And then Ellen had to leave and I assumed it was to go set up for dinner. I was dying to hear more—I hadn't really heard anything yet—but I was also wiped. Practically before the sounds of her feet retreating on the footpath faded, I was into a deep, cold-ridden sleep. I kept dreaming the same thing over and over again—that I'd been hired to clean the windows on Ellis Bell's four-storey house—and just as I got my first glimpse of him, I'd wake up. My mouth would be all sticky-dry from breathing through it. I'd try to blow but nothing would come out, there'd just be a minor popping sensation somewhere behind my ears and the effort of blowing would give me a headache. Then I'd nod off again, get the job, get my pail and squeegee, and just as I was about to do a final vinegar and newspaper rinse (my mum insists on it), there would be Ellis, walking into the living room looking so perfectly dreamy yet unaware of his dreaminess, and even though I'm in coveralls and tee shirt I'm looking very attractive myself, and unaware of my attractiveness. Then, just as he walks in and glances up I wake up—mouth sticky, miserable—and go through my whole routine again.

FOURTEEN

ELLEN DIDN'T COME BACK that night, just Cathy with a thermos of chicken noodle soup. I remember that during the night, as I was making my way to the nearest porta-potty, both nostrils cleared for a moment and it was glorious. Unfortunately it didn't last, but it was a breakthrough. I stood for a while in my pyjamas looking up through the trees at an incredibly clear and beautiful sky. You just don't get to see the stars like that when you live in town. Light pollution. Sometimes, when Ellis Bell has made a house call to someone in distress, he comes out of their house and looks up at the sky and we can see everything—the big dipper, and a bunch of constellations—which just would not be the case in real life in a town the size of Willow Heights. I don't care. That's what they do in TV and movies. For instance, sometimes, apparently, if the scene is in the wilderness, the soundtrack will have the call of a loon on it even though there would be no loons actually found in that place, wherever it's supposed to be. That's showbiz. I never get too picky about stuff like that, I'd rather get all caught up in the story than say, "Aha! In the last scene he had a blue shirt and now it's white," or "There was a bowl of fruit on the coffee table and now it's flowers."

Ellen noticed everything, even in real life, which is what made her a good storyteller, I guess. She noticed little personal habits that people had and she could imitate them perfectly, which was a laugh. She could do Tara pushing her hand through her short short hair, Cathy's lips pressed together, Todd's eager Archie Andrews look on his face. She even imitated the holiday dads trying to hang around Cliff while he hammered or sawed something and Cliff's scowl as he brushed them off like flies.

"Whadabowme?" I said, the next time she came.

She did an imitation of me with my cold— droopy eyelids, mouth open, saggy body—but she was more interested in talking about Cate.

"Cate's got a crush on Tara," she said.

"Whadyuhmean?"

"Watches her, like—" and here she did an imitation of Cate's intense stare "—when she thinks no one's looking."

"Rilly?"

I'm ashamed now at how interested and excited I was by this idea.

"Did you know Tara was sort of adopted?"

I didn't.

"Yeah. Last night we were, like, getting ready for lights out and she goes, 'My bio-dad something or rather,' and I'm, like, 'Your what?' and Cate goes, 'Figure it out.'"

"Thass three words," I said.

"Hey, yeah!" Ellen said."So then Tara tells how she's got a bio-dad and her dad-dad raised her but she's known about the bio-dad forever and he lives just, like, in the next town or something."

Was that why Tara seemed so much calmer than me? She had an extra dad?

"So today Cate's watching her like—" Ellen imitated Cate again "—even when everyone's looking."

"Rilly?"

"You can't help who you fall in love with."

This made me feel squirmy. Not that Cate might actually be a lesbian—I couldn't care less—but that you couldn't help who you fell in love with. Was it really possible to, say, just go *boing!* instantly for some guy? What if he turned out to be a serial murderer—would you still be in love? Haven't you noticed, for instance, that there are people you find instantly attractive but then when you get to know them a little and don't actually like them you can't see it anymore? Then there are people you wouldn't ever have looked at but you get to know them and like them and then you find them really good looking? That's always how it is for me, anyway.

Ellen glanced at her watch. "Yikes, I'm outta here."

I felt awful. She'd spent the whole time catching me up on what had gone on at the lodge when what I really wanted to hear about was what went on at Ellis Bell's. Plus, hearing about the lodge only made me feel guilty for not being there and doing my job.

"Finished?" She was pointing to the chicken soup thermos. I nodded. "Take it back for ya."

And then she straightened my cot again and tucked me in and I suddenly felt so tired all I wanted to do was sleep. I don't know how long I slept, but when I next woke up I could breathe through my right nostril! Oh, that felt good. Then I realized it was because I was lying on my left side, so I rolled over onto my right and, sure enough, in moments the snot that was clogging my sinuses followed and my left nostril cleared. There was a moment there during the transfer when both sides were clear and I inhaled a lovely big breath, but it didn't last. Still, that didn't matter; if I had just one available nostril it meant I could close my mouth but still breathe and that was so wonderful I fell fast asleep again, only waking up once—at the point where Ellis glanced up from his living room and instead of being in my cute coveralls I felt a horrible embarrassment because I suddenly realized that (after trying on and rejecting endless combinations) I'd forgotten to dress at all that day and there I was washing Ellis Bell's windows naked.

FIFTEEN

ELLEN WOULD PROBABLY be setting up for dinner, then serving dinner, so I certainly didn't expect to see her again that day. Imagine my excitement when I heard her steps on the path. I'd been awake for a while and debating whether to flip through the magazines she'd left me or just keep drifting in and out of sleep. It's amazing how you can sleep so much during the day when you're sick and then still sleep at night too.

"Snothead, how ya doin'?"

Now, I was actually feeling quite a bit better but I didn't want to let on in case it would make her cut her mercy visit short.

"Cathy was gonna bring this, but I nabbed it."

From her backpack she lifted a little box that probably smelled wonderful to people whose smellers were fully functional.

"Leftovers."

I tucked in, which was a signal to Ellen that I was no longer at death's door.

"Now," she said, when I'd finished, "maybe you're

ready for a little expedition." She reached into her backpack and pulled out my anorak. "Thought you might wanna get outta this crappy room for once."

I did. I pulled the anorak over my pyjamas and stuffed a handful of tissues in my pocket before heading out the door. It felt good to be upright and in the fresh night air. There was just a glimmer of light behind the mountains and a few really brilliant stars in the sky. The tide was high. We went down to the end of the wharf and sat with our backs leaning against the big chest that held life jackets and preservers. It was dark enough that a few lights were starting to twinkle on Ellis Bell's island. I imagined him sitting at his desk turning on his reading lamp or maybe eating at the big dining room table underneath the fabulous chandelier that the Gurings had given them for their wedding present. He'd be sitting there, hoping for a kind word from Arabella, when she'd start in at him about something or someone in town that had offended her that day.

"You wanna go?" Ellen asked.

By the way she said it I knew she wasn't asking if I wanted to go back to the ice house but if I wanted to go to the island.

"Oh! No. I don't know. Yeah. But I'd be too scared. They probably come here to get away from fans like me."

"Aha!"

Darn. I'd still been sort of pretending that I was only interested in this because of my mum's crush and now I'd given it away that I was a real fan after all. Oh, what did it matter?

"Anyways, if someone's not watching them, they don't know they exist."

"That's not very nice."

She looked at me strangely.

"Feel sorry for the kids," she said, "'specially the little boy, he's a sweetie. The girl's a sulker, but by the end I felt sorry for her too."

"Would you have stayed on? Taken a year off before college or anything?"

"They asked me."

"Wow!"

"Yeah. 'Cause everyone could see the kids were different with me, but no way. Not that I'm crazy about the college idea, or anything, but looking after kids?"

"Tiring," I said, thinking of my munchkins at the lodge.

"Exhausting," she said. "And kinda sad."

Then she was in storytelling mode again and I got to just lean back, look out at my dream island, and listen.

"Marie goes to get the kids to introduce me and I'm wondering how I'm gonna *be* in this super clean house. I mean, no stains, no dust bunnies anywhere.

I'm comparing it to my own house—we're talking mess, I am so not into tidy—when she comes in with the children."

"They both, like, hang back, but then I see this flower in the little guy's hand and I'm like, aw. He must've picked it from some vase on his way to see me and I just break into this big grin and thank him and sniff it and all those things you do when some little kid does something cute for you. So Eddie and I hit it off, but Belle looks at me, like, who are *you*? And says, 'I don't like your face.' Marie starts in with 'Now, Belle,' and then, as if, she, like, remembers who these kids *are*, she drops that attitude and just switches to saying how lovely my face is and all that crap and this kid and me have locked eyes and it's all I can do not to say something nasty back—"

"You shouldn't," I interrupted.

"Yeah, yeah, I know. Kids, huh? I'm supposed to be Miss Perfect Nanny and say something like, 'Well, I like your face, Belle,' but I don't, okay? I glare at her. She's six, she's old enough to know— oh, quit giving me that look—anyways, haven't you even noticed that these people named their kids after themselves? Only cutsie poo—little Edgar is actually christened Ed and little Isobel is actually christened Belle—and they're obviously adopted."

"How do you know?" I didn't remember any of

this from my magazines, but they tended to focus on the show, not real life.

"They're from one of those *ia* countries— Rumania, Bulgaria, Serbia, whatever—and they really were brother and sister."

"That's so nice!"

"That's what I thought, so I only glare at the little brat and don't mouth off. I figure a few days of my kind attention and she'll be putty in my hands, but she turns out to be a tough case. These kids had been with the Lintons since Eddie was a baby and Belle was two—but Sarah," she interrupted herself, "you must be wiped sitting out here, maybe we oughta get you back to bed."

I shook my head. Actually, the night air was penetrating my sinuses more than I wanted to admit.

"At least I can jump ahead and not bore you with every little—"

"No! I like your details, they help me picture everything in my mind."

So she sat back on the log and started into her story again.

"Marie disappears because these aren't the only peoples' lives she organizes and I'm, like, 'What now?' I don't know where anything is in this house, I don't know anybody in this house, and there are these two rug rats looking at me and I'm thinking, *Am I at work now? Like, on duty or what?* Surely Mom's gonna walk in and say, 'Oh, you've met the children,' and take me up to my gorgeous room to unpack and freshen up. I've always wanted to freshen up, but no."

"So there I am and I'm tryna think fast and it comes to me...what do you do with any normal kid, right? You ask to see their room and then they show you their toys and before long you're on the floor doing dolls or trucks and the natural kid energy takes care of the awkward stuff. So Eddie takes my hand and leads me to the stairs and sulky Belle follows behind, only first she goes, she goes, 'Are you going to just leave your bag in our living room?' Part of me wants to grab up my stuff and lug it around till someone shows me where I'll be sleeping, but I think, *Okay, you've got to establish early on with this brat that you're no pushover,* so I look at my bag and I look at her and I go, 'Yeah.' Then Eddie takes my hand and we head upstairs."

"The staircase isn't especially grand or anything, but it's wide and there's a landing at the top with a railing and a big rectangular mirror just at the top of the stairs so I can see us as we're coming up the last few steps. We take a left and go along the landing to another set of stairs, just normal ones, and this leads to the kid floor."

"The kid floor?"

"Uh huh. They get a whole floor to themselves.

So we go into Eddie's room, which is, like, huge and has two sets of bunk beds—"

"Two?"

"Yeah, and first I'm thinking sleepovers, right? And I'm seeing all these little guys in their baseball jammies and whatnot. But Eddie's only four, and you don't start having sleepovers till—what, eight or something. So then I'm thinking you got a space that size you gotta fill it, right? So there's two sets of bunk beds, and one of those couches that's really a folded-over double bed and it has these humongous cushions piled on it. There's a train set that takes up half the room. I mean you've never seen so much tiny track in your life."

I cringed. I knew just the kind of toy she was describing, where there's absolutely nothing for the kid to do or imagine because everything's done for him. There would be little cows grazing, or lying down in fields, and little depots with boxes marked "flour" and "milk" to be loaded on to boxcars. And everything would be perfect and realistic looking.

"So Eddie sees I'm not wild about his room—"

"Kids sense everything."

"So he goes, 'Wanna see Belle's room?' and I go, 'Sure,' and we walk the length of their floor to Belle's room."

"Let me guess," I said. "Princess."

"Oh, man."

I didn't say so but I felt all this would be Isobel's doing. Ellis was very down to earth and wouldn't want his kids in rooms like that.

"We're talking the works. Canopy bed with a trundle bed under that, we're talking—"

"Barbie."

"Barbie. A vanity, a ballet barre, a walk-in closet, the whole schmeer, and this kid, Belle, is like the toughest little kid, right? Her family back in Bulmania could probably live in the dollhouse in this room. So, what do I say? I mean, already I don't like her, but I can't hurt her feelings with 'It sucks,' right?"

"No!"

"So I don't say a thing. But she knows, and those dark eyes glare out at me from beneath black bangs and I'm thinking of all those movies where, like, the spoiled kid turns out to be Satan—"

"Ellen…"

"I know, I know, but I'm alone far from home and I want my mommy. Thank god at this real tense moment I hear movement somewhere in the house. The kids hear it too and it breaks some kind of spell and Belle looks a little less satanic and all our eyes are on the floor while our ears listen and, somehow, in the way kids know, there's some sound that tells them it's not just another staffer.

"'Daddy!' Eddie yells and he tears out into the hall."

SIXTEEN

JUST AS I WAS ABOUT to finally get my first "real life" glimpse of Ellis Bell I had a coughing fit. There was no stopping me, even though it was an unsatisfying dry cough. Once the tickle mechanism in my throat was triggered, I hacked and hacked, only pausing to catch my breath and swear I wouldn't cough again, but being absolutely unable to resist the urge to clear that tickle away for good just one last time. When I finally did stop my head was aching as badly as after a prolonged nose blow. And my throat was raw. What I really needed was a spoonful of honey to coat my throat, or a good gargle with vinegar, but I had a cough drop in my pyjama pocket. As I peeled off the wrapper my hands were actually a little shaky from all the coughing.

"Y'okay?"

Poor Ellen. At least she hadn't tried to do anything, which only makes it worse.

"I'm okay, I'm okay," I whispered, sucking like mad to get the first precious trickle of cough drop going.

"Wanna go back?"

I shook my head. I was not going to be interrupted on the brink of meeting Ellis Bell in real life, but my whole body felt momentarily boneless. And my head was throbbing.

"Want anything?"

I swallowed a mouthful of cough drop juice. "There's aspirin in the ice house. I think it's awhile since I've had any."

"Hot lemon?"

"Would you mind?"

She went to the ice house and came back with my aspirin first, bless her. I always take aspirin dry anyway and actually like the taste when I'm feeling sick. What I don't like are those coated aspirins or anything that's "timed release." Who wants little drug bombs going off throughout the day? Just take your medicine and let your body do its work. I feel like "timed release" sits in my stomach and dissolves so slowly that it's pooped out before it's done any good.

But that's neither here nor there; what's interesting is that Ellen was actually pretty good at taking care of people, so I revised my feelings about her being a nanny. I mean, all it takes is putting yourself in someone else's place and trying to imagine what you would be like in that situation.

She came back from the lodge with a blanket draped around her neck the way Ellis Bell wears his stethoscope, a thermos mug of hot lemon for me and cocoa for her (you know you're sick when you'd rather have the hot lemon) and after tucking the blanket around me and handing me my drink she put hers down on the wharf and proceeded to pull all kinds of stuff from various pockets: a bunch of those little cracker packets you get with soup, individually wrapped rectangles of hard cheese (Cathy never stocked the processed slices or the cheese strings, which I actually would have preferred) and, best of all, a little package of honey from the breakfast jam basket. She even brought a tiny spoon to scoop it out with. For all her tough talk, she was really pretty considerate underneath. She just knew, once I'd had my honey and half the hot lemon, that the best thing for me would be distraction from my misery, and she went right back into the story.

"So I'm still on the stairs when I see little Eddie, like, *fly* into his dad's arms and Linton catches him and says, 'What's up, doc?' to Eddie and 'How's my girl?' to Belle."

That's just what he says to the kids on the pediatric ward at WHGH.

"Then, this is my big moment, right? He'll look up and see me on the stairs and our eyes will, like, lock, and he'll know I'm the one for him and he'll leave Isobel and run off with me."

Ellis Bell would never do that.

"Doesn't even notice me. I'm, like, *hello?*"

"What about the kids?"

"Eddie's too excited to remember, and Belle hates me from the start so she's ignoring me. I mean, any normal dad and I'd've gone right up and said 'Hi, I'm Ellen,' but he's not normal, so I just freeze on the stairs there and the three of them go out somewhere and I don't unfreeze till they're gone."

"That's weird."

"Tell me about it. I hear a car start up and drive off and I'm, like, 'Excuse me? I'm all alone in this humongous house…where's my room? There's nothing to eat…' I'm, like, *Okay, don't panic, El, it's not like they've left you in the middle of the rainforest or anything*, then I hear a car pull up and I'm going, *Yes! They've come back for me* and all of a sudden I love this job, but it's not them and in walks this woman—"

"Arabella."

"Isobel, you goof, and Marie is with her, ticking things into her Palm Pilot. Marie notices me. I'm telling you, these people could have a houseful of weirdos and they'd never know. If you're not one of them you're, like, the help, right? Invisible.

So Marie goes, 'Oh, Ellen, there you are. Let me introduce you to Mrs. Linton.'"

The name jarred me because, again, I was visualizing his wife in the TV show.

"So Marie introduces us and I'm, like, 'Nice to meet you,' and she goes, she goes, 'I hope you can last the summer,' and then she's going on about some appointment or other to Marie and I'm like, *hello?*"

"That's so much like Arabella Guring!"

Arabella was always planning parties or scheming. She never even listened when Ellis came home all sad because he'd lost a patient. In the early stages of their marriage he'd try to make her understand—or at least think about someone other than herself for a change—but now he goes to the willow trees and leans up against them and gives himself time to process the whole thing before even going home.

According to Ellen, Isobel was just as full of herself as Arabella. Ellis didn't seem to spend too much time at the house even though he was on hiatus from *Willow Heights* and it was summer.

"Fast forward. I've been there, what, four weeks almost. Half through. We get our routine down pat and all and I'm startin' to feel not just okay with the job but real good about it, you know? I can, like, get the kids to do stuff, which you could just tell was way more than any other nanny could do. So I'm feelin' on top a things and that's when I start overhearin' the fights."

"Fights?"

"Her and him. Well, her mostly, he's, like, real quiet. But it's like she thinks he's fightin' with her, 'cause what you hear is *her* screechin' like he's just called her a rotten name or somethin'. She goes, 'Don't look at me that way,' and there's not a sound, only then she starts up again, 'Like I'm *beneath* you,' so maybe he was going, 'What way?' I dunno. I thought she was just a nutbar, but when you think about it he might have been givin' her little pokes but so quietly you wouldn't know.

"So she goes, 'like I'm *beneath* you. *All that again*, as you dismiss it, is part of my *life*, you know.' Okay, and then he *must* have said something, 'cause she just went ballistic on him. She goes—all screechy— she goes, 'You cruel vile brute, I was young—just a girl!'"

"Yuck."

"I know, eh?"

"What did she mean 'all that again'?"

Ellen just shrugged.

"Now she's all wound up and she goes, 'I loved you, Edgar Linton, and I'd have done anything for you. If it weren't for me you'd be *nothing*. Your high-and-mighty parents disowned you but because you wanted to be something as ridiculous as an actor. You ran away from them and you came back because you'd run out of money, you'd gone to Halifax, Toronto, Montreal, and no one had hired you, not even as an extra. You seemed so glamorous to me—the beautiful Edgar Linton, so witty, all the girls in love with you, you could have done anything and you dropped out of high school to pursue your dream. Do you remember what it was like when you came crawling back? They made you feel like a failure! Only *me* believing in you—' and he must've said something, 'cause she goes, 'Yes, the love of a good woman! How dare you!' and I think she must've started whackin' on him at that point 'cause I heard thump thump sounds."

"You're kidding."

"Nope. From the sounds of it, though, it was just a pillow or something—flump, flump, you know?"

"Still."

"She was pretty worked up."

"Over what, though?"

"Okay, here's what I figure. They've known each other since like, forever. She loves him from afar, he's the Guy Most Likely to Whatever, and she's just this sludgie—"

"Sludgie?"

"Yeah, you know, those kids you're supposed to be nice to, but they're always kinda miserable and hangin' around and you're always tryna ditch 'em? So he defies the folks and goes off to be a star only he can't act—"

"Hey!" I was thinking of the episode where he had to tell Mark he was HIV positive.

"Chill, okay? He comes home, everyone's all sneery, only little Isobel looks up at him like he's this amazing creature and because no one else is even talking to him and she's filled out a little now—" Ellen was starting to sound more like me concocting one of my scenarios "—they have sex, she thinks she owns him, they get married—"

I couldn't resist joining in. "They run off to Hollywood together," I said. "She gets a job as a waitress—"

"Pays for his acting lessons," Ellen said, "photos…the nose job—"

"What?"

"Kidding. She works double shifts, he auditions."

"For the part of Ellis Bell."

"And the rest, as they say, is history."

"Only…"

"Why all the misery?"

I nodded. How could such a romantic beginning turn so sour?

"'Cause they're both miserable people." I made a face at her. "I dunno. Why is *anyone* miserable?"

This was one of those discussions that made me uncomfortable—like not being able to help who you fall in love with. Did miserable people just turn miserable overnight? There had to be some point, or series of points, where you could catch yourself and stop it.

Apparently Ellen overheard two more fights and they were exactly the same.

"Like an endless loop," she said, "'round and 'round."

Only there were a few more nasty tidbits. He said she was raised in a "hovel" and she said he had "ice water in his veins." He said she ignored the children and she burst into tears and called him all kinds of unprintable names. Pretty ugly stuff. Then there was one more incident Ellen wanted to tell me, she said, that might make me feel differently towards Ellis Bell, if I didn't already.

SEVENTEEN

THE STORY HAD TO WAIT, though, because it was getting late. As we packed up to go we kept looking over at the island—plenty of lights were twinkling on it now—wondering if they were over there fighting with each other.

Once back in my little cot I fell into the first good sleep I'd had since catching the cold. When I woke up the next morning I realized that I'd simply have to get back to work the next day. Even if I spent the whole day sniffling, I'd feel too guilty to miss any more time. That meant that I had one last chance to hear Ellen's stories uninterrupted.

In many ways that was the hardest day yet, because I actually felt well enough to get up but I didn't, I just stayed in the little ice house reading magazines over and over again and waiting for Ellen to tell me about the final incident that would change my attitude towards Ellis Bell. It did kind of chill me. I tried to justify it to myself by thinking that he's an actor after all and that his craft is a large part of what he's about. Still, I can't get it out of my head.

It happened after Ellen had been with them almost the whole summer. She'd managed to get both kids playing real kid games—blocks, colouring, Hide and Seek (they loved Hide and Seek)—instead of always just watching a screen or letting some toy have all the fun.

"So it's Hide and Seek again and I'm It. So, okay, so the way little Eddie plays, he runs into a corner or a cupboard or something and I go, 'Ready or not you must be caught, come out come out wherever you are!' and then I'm looking and I go, 'Are you under the sofa?' and he goes, 'No!' 'Are you behind the curtain?' And the whole time I'm doing this I'm, like, actually looking in these spots and he's giggling and' calling out 'No,' and just dying to get caught until finally he goes, 'I'm in the corner!' or whatever and I find him and he giggles and it starts all over again."

"So we'd got to this point where Eddie'd actually hide and not let on and this was, like, a major leap in game playing for the little guy, so I'm in the front hall looking for him and all of a sudden he just can't bear it any more and he runs out from his hiding spot and tears across the hall and, like, trips so bad I see his little nose go smack onto that hard floor."

Her face squinched up as she told me about it.

"He's down and I'm like, oh god, he's not only not making a sound, which is bad enough, he's not *moving.* So I let out this piercing scream—'Eddie!'—I mean, really, I've never heard myself sound like that before. I thought maybe he was dead, it was that awful."

"Scary."

"Terrifying. Then as I'm kneeling over little Eddie—and I'm going 'Help, somebody, *help* me!' I hear someone running like mad from upstairs and I look—"

She was acting this all out now, kneeling down with Eddie, looking up at the landing.

"And there's Edgar, peering over the railing with this awful look on his face, I mean, he's so worried he looks phoney, you know? His mouth's all gaping and his eyes're all buggy. Then he starts running for the stairs and—here's the part I can't get out of my head—"

Me neither.

"—he turns for a moment to look at himself in the mirror. Yeah. Right then, when he's thinking maybe his kid's dead, he takes a moment to turn and look in that mirror and it's like, 'Oh, this is how a person looks when he's devastated…tuck *that* away, might need *that* expression someday.' Then he's, like, downstairs with me and Eddie in no time flat."

"Ewww."

"Times ten. Freaky, freaky, freaky. And I'm, like, simultaneously registering this and wondering if

Eddie's okay and wondering if Edgar's even aware that he *did* that and suddenly he's like, 'What happened? What did you do?'"

"What did you do?"

"Yeah! I'm like, excuse me? Listen, Bub, this is *your* kid I been lookin' after here and I'm worried sick enough not to bother checkin' out how I look in the mirror, now what's with this what did *I* do?"

"Good for you!"

"Nah, I didn't really say any of that, I'm like, all shaky and worried and upset and I just keep going, 'Nothing, nothing,' and finally all kinds of people start zooming in from other rooms and an ambulance is called and they start doing things like taking his pulse and listening for breathing—all those things that Linton and I just didn't think to do—and little Eddie starts to revive, thank god, and I start to cry out of relief. And before I know it, it's all over. Eddie's, like, gone off in the ambulance and his dad's with him and everyone's back to work and I'm like, 'Uh—did this happen or what?'"

"Didn't anyone—?"

"Nope. No sandwich and tea, no 'Poor Ellen, you must've been so worried,' no nothing."

"Sheesh."

"And I never saw Eddie again."

"What?"

"Never saw Belle or Isobel, never saw *any* of

them. A taxi came to take me to the airport and that was it. So long. One thing I *will* say, they paid me the same bucks as if I'd stayed the whole summer, but, Gandhi."

I really hated it when Ellen said "Gandhi" like that for "gone," but I didn't say anything because the story she'd just told was such an awful thing to have happened. They never even gave her a chance to explain her side of things. It seemed so mean. And since little Eddie was genuinely fond of her it seemed awfully mean to him, too.

"That's how people like that are. You're hired, you don't work out, you're fired."

"But you did work out!"

"Not if Eddie smashed his nose."

"It's so unfair."

"Yeah, well, that's why I'll never do a nanny gig again. Not because I wouldn't get a reference from those creeps, but because it's too sad. Munchkins get attached and then, poof, Gandhi."

This time I did wince.

"Excuse *me*. Hey, I forgot to tell you, your folks are coming. Next weekend. Too bad 'cause it's, like, the first time you and me would've had time off together."

She'd reached into her pocket and pulled out a printed-off email. There was no need for me to read it because she'd already told me the news.

"How did you know my password?"

"Sarah, Babes, gotcha on the second try." She held out her left hand and bent back her fingers with her right. "First try—Ellis Bell. Second—Bell Ellis. Piece of cake."

EIGHTEEN

ELLEN WAS STARTING to get to me. Infiltrating someone's email—wasn't that a federal offense? Part of me knew that it was that kind of chutzpah that made her fun to be around, but another part was suddenly furious and wanted to scream.

She got all defensive and we had one of those arguments where neither of us was quite sure how it started or what it was initially about. I can't believe I wasted my visiting time over something like that, but I did, and before I knew it she was off and I figured she'd punish me by not coming back again.

I was right.

And that was real punishment, too, because I was feeling much better. Every time I blew my nose now I got a big clot of yellow snot and it was very satisfying. I was starting to get sick of dumb magazines. Could it be that in less than a month at CC Lodge I, too, was losing my taste for popular culture? I didn't want to see the latest fashions, or determine my face shape, or learn how to correct my figure flaws with the right bathing suit. I just wanted to hear more stories about Ellen's time with the Lintons and gossip from around the lodge—did Cate have a crush on Tara, was Cliff hypnotizing lobsters? Tune in tomorrow.

That night, completely by accident, I tuned into something I'll never forget. I was on my way to the porta-potty when I saw, through the trees but clear in the moonlight, the silhouette of Cliff. He was standing beside the big birch tree that grew beside the office. I can see it now in my mind's eye like that shadow art that people have on their lawns at home. Usually there's the figure of an old man with a pipe in his mouth, or a girl with a ponytail waving her hand. When you drive by, it always gives you a little pause because it looks sort of real; then when you actually look at it, it's clearly shadow art. This scene was like that. Tree, man, small house. Instantly I realized that if he looked up, there was a chance he'd see me that way: girl, jammies, porta-potty. So, in order not to seem like I was spying, I kept going, though I may have tiptoed. My hand was on the door. If I'd just opened the door then it would have made the springy noise it always makes and he'd have known someone was there and the next thing wouldn't have happened. Instead, I hesitated and behind me I heard the strangest sound. With my hand still on the door handle I turned around and saw, I swear to god this time I wasn't dreaming, Cliff bashing his head up against the tree. Honest. He'd wrapped his hands around the trunk and was banging his head, again and again. Just when I thought I'd burst, another silhouette appeared—Cathy in a dressing gown. The gown flapped behind her as she rushed towards Cliff. I expected him to shout and maybe storm off, maybe right past me so that he could go wandering on the mountain the way Tara had seen him that time, but he did just the opposite of what I expected. He sort of flung himself at Cathy and gathered her up in his arms. They formed one big silhouette there, locked together, and it sounded to me like he was crying.

Cliff crying? It was so…un-Cliff.

Poor Cathy. She must have been nearly squished to death in those big beefy arms. Suddenly the silhouette had two heads and I guess she'd managed to work her arms free. It looked like she must have been holding his face in her hands and saying something very intently. I strained to make out what it was but all I could hear was the word "not" because she'd emphasized it enough for me to hear it over his sobs.

By the time they finally left, Cliff still clinging to Cathy with both his arms around her like he was hanging on for dear life, I had to go so badly I couldn't just open the door and step inside. I waited a while, doubled over, until that moment when I knew I'd be able to get in, drop my pyjamas, and sit down without wetting myself.

I made it. That was the longest pee of my life. Sitting there, with the nauseating cake of air freshener in the urinal, it occurred to me that I would have preferred an outhouse. I was getting pretty sick of these plastic porta-potties—they certainly weren't "in keeping" with the landscape which is why they were always out of the way—and, also, if it had been an outhouse with normal hinges, maybe I'd have been able to watch that whole scene from the little crescent-shaped window instead of staying frozen to the spot outside at night in the dark in my pyjamas.

When I'd finished and was outside again I looked down at the scene. There was the birch and the office in the moonlight, no big deal. I let my eyes take in as much of the place as they could from that spot. There was the path that led from the office into the main part of the lodge, the roofs of a few small guest cabins, the wharf. I was mad at myself for fighting with Ellen because I was dying to tell her what I'd seen. Then, just as I was imagining her face reacting to all that I had to tell her, I remembered how she'd casually reached into her pocket to hand over my personal email and it made me mad at her all over again. It would be delicious to know this information about Cathy and Cliff, and to know how much Ellen would love to hear it, and to not tell. These were my thoughts as I started back along the footpath.

Outside the house I stopped and stretched and looked up at the mountain. Some nights it was so wild and crazy up there you would swear the trees would be toppled over the next morning, but that night it was beautiful and there was the softest breeze blowing. Tara said, and it made sense, that big, jagged mountains like the Rockies or the Alps look impressive, but they're new. These mountains, she said, were part of the Appalachians. They'd been tall and jagged millions of years ago, but had been worn down and rounded over time. Just looking at them was, in a way, like looking millions of years into the past. And for all we knew the stars above might have gone out years ago, but because they were so far away their light was just reaching earth now.

It made me feel very grown up to be out there like that at night, contemplating the sky and the mountains. No one, not even my parents, knew exactly where I was at that moment in time. Pretty amazing. I must have been staring up into space feeling pleased with myself for quite a while, because I felt suddenly chilled and surely, even in Cape Breton, the wind didn't pick up that fast.

With one last glance at the mountain in its relatively calm state I went back into the ice house, pulled the extra blanket over my sleeping bag, and shivered as the wind, then rain, pounded the shingles.

NINETEEN

THERE WAS A KNOCK on my door and then it was pushed open just a little and I saw Cathy's tired face peeking in.

"Oh dear, I woke you, Sarah."

"No," I said, pushing myself up on my elbow. "I was already awake."

By the light outside and the sounds I guessed it was about ten o'clock.

"I just wondered if Cate might be here."

She didn't know her own daughter very well if she believed that Cate might be visiting me. Cate barely spoke to me. But then, how was Cathy to know that? For all she knew, we were gabbing away and having a fine old time in our cabin every night. Suddenly I felt very sorry for Cathy. She'd had Cliff to cope with last night and then woken up to find Cate had gone missing again.

"I'll do prep," I said.

"What?"

I'd already thrown off my sleeping bag and was standing up. "I'm feeling way better today. Honest."

"That wasn't why I…are you sure?"

"Sure I'm sure. I just need to have a shower and dress. I'll be there soon."

Water pressure or no water pressure, that was the best shower of my life. I washed my hair, I trimmed my nails, I flossed and brushed. I even brushed my tongue. I was having one of those energy bursts that come after a cold and I practically over to the lodge. I was actually looking forward to it since a) I'd never worked there before and b) people wouldn't have very big expectations for me since I was just pitching in and helping out until Cate came back. Also, I was grateful to have a chance to help Cathy out after being such a slug for the last few days. Plus Ellen might be doing prep too or at the very least would be coming into the kitchen over and over again to pick up her orders and, when I decided the moment was right, I'd glance up and we'd make eye contact and burst out laughing over something and then we'd be back to being buddies and everything would be great between us again and I'd tell her about last night. That was the fantasy. The reality was much less interesting.

First of all, the reason it's called prep is that you're preparing things for the cooks and so you're there ahead of everyone, including the wait staff. About half an hour into topping and chopping Arvi came over and put her hand on my shoulder.

"You got the hang of this very quickly, Sarah," she said. "Perhaps you and your friend should trade places more often."

Naturally, I thought that she, like Cathy, had assumed Cate and I were on friendlier terms than we were, but it turned out she was talking about Ellen after all. That's right, while I'd been sick as a dog, Ellen had infiltrated more than my email— she'd infiltrated my job. Apparently Arvi and Cathy had already had a discussion about the fact that it would be hard on some of the kids if I were to get well before their week was over because they'd become so "attached" to dear old Ellen. Hadn't she said she'd never work with kids again for just that reason? Hadn't she also led me to believe they were dreadfully short-handed without me?

When I was five years old and had started school full time, my mum got into workaholic mode. Dad had a little sign printed up that read, "The graveyard is filled with indispensable people." Mum put it in a magnetic frame and stuck it on the fridge, where it remains to this day. Every time I get a snack I see that sign—along with several pictures of myself at various ages and stages of cuteness—but as if any of that matters. The point I'm trying to make is not that I was so disappointed that the place didn't fall apart without me, but that I was getting more and more ticked at Ellen.

"Who's doing Ellen's job?" I asked.

"Joanne Dunphy," Arvi said.

The muffin woman. Why didn't they get the muffin woman to do my job?

It was easy enough for Ellen and me to avoid each other the entire day. Cathy came to check in with me occasionally and ask how I was feeling, but I think she was really trying to find out if anyone had seen Cate. This was the longest time she'd gone missing.

I actually started to have a little fun in the kitchen by dinnertime, especially with Marsha and Jason and Todd. Since dessert that night was especially fancy, they needed all four of us to plate it and, fortunately for me, lobster wasn't on the menu so I didn't have to see Cliff hypnotizing them.

By nighttime I was very tired. Not only had I lost the energy high from being over my cold, but I'd worked long hours and been on my feet all day. When Tara and I got back to the cabin Ellen was already in bed with her back to us. I doubt that she was asleep.

"Do your feet hurt?" I asked Tara.

"Not anymore," she said. "You get used to it. And we get more days off than you."

It was true I just had Sundays off—the turnaround day for guests—but at least I knew I had every Sunday. They worked four-, five-, and six-day rotations.

"I'm not complaining," I said. "I really enjoyed working in the kitchen."

That was said for Ellen's benefit. I didn't want her thinking that I cared that she'd stolen my job.

"It's nice to have you back, Sarah," Tara said. "We missed you in this cabin, didn't we?"

There was no reply.

"I guess Ellen's asleep," Tara whispered.

I knew she wasn't, but I also knew how to find out. Gossip. The bunk below Tara's was still empty.

"So," I whispered. "Any idea where Cate went?"

"Mm. Not really."

"What do you mean, 'not really'?" I figured Ellen must be dying of curiosity.

"Well, she's already back."

"She is?"

"I saw her on the road when you and I were walking here."

Well, if that wasn't enough to make Ellen perk up—the idea that Cate was on her way back and might walk into the cabin at any moment—I don't know what was. I could feel her listening but she didn't move a muscle.

It was very tempting to let Tara know what I'd seen the night before but suddenly I didn't want Ellen to have the satisfaction of pretending to be asleep and yet hearing every word.

Two could play this game.

TWENTY

THE NEXT DAY I slept in. I guess getting over a cold, learning a new job, and being mad at Ellen was pretty tiring. There was no one in the cabin but me. I hadn't heard Cate come in at night—if she had come in—and I hadn't heard any of them get up and off in the morning. After dressing and washing I headed down towards the lodge for breakfast. From there I could see the little kids, and Ellen, busy, sailing stick boats to the pond. That had been my idea. You put them in just under the waterfall and see how they get stuck and unstuck on the rocks and moss in the feeder stream. Once they've made their way to the "ocean" you lift them out and start again. Squeals of delight could be heard each time a little kid let go of his or her stick. Ellen looked up and I looked away and kept walking.

On the verandah of the lodge I met both Cathy and Cliff. They were having an intense conversation and it would have been easy to slip past them without interacting and go inside, but Cathy beckoned to me.

"How are you feeling today, Sarah?"

"Better, thanks."

Then, thinking that "better" could be construed as better but not completely well, I ran on a bit.

"Better than better, I mean. I'm all better. I'm well."

Now, I didn't find that such a strange response but apparently to the person who called me "Sarah Sarah Lockwood from New Brunswick," it was.

"Ha!" he said.

The man didn't chuckle softly—*ha, ha, ha*—it was one loud and sharp ha! that made me almost jump to hear it. I was trying to figure out whether it was a friendly *ha!* or a *ha!* of disgust or, worse, actually an *aha!* as in, "*Aha!* You are better, you slacker," when Cathy, as usual, rescued the situation.

"We're just tired, Sarah," she said. "We didn't get much sleep last night."

Actually, it was the night before last that they'd missed their sleep because Cliff was out bashing his head against a tree, and according to my dad's marathon theory that's why they would be tired and grumpy. Mind you, Cliff always seemed grumpy to me, and according to Cathy they really hadn't got much sleep the night before either.

"Cate came back very late," she said.

"I know," I said. "Tara saw—"

"Tara," Cliff cut me off, wincing. "That's the one with the mouth—"

"No, darling," Cathy interrupted. "Ellen's the funny one."

A sharp nod was Cliff's response.

"Speaking of Ellen," Cathy said to me, "Did Arvi mention the idea of her finishing out your shift this week, Sarah?"

"Yes," I said.

I thought I could sense Cliff sneering behind that black beard so I tried to appear casual about the whole job-swapping thing, though I didn't like it one bit.

"Then you have today off," Cathy announced.

According to the rotation schedule it was actually Cate's day off. This didn't make me at all happy. My post-cold energy burst had me raring to go. What I really wanted to do was get the kids making a walk-in castle out of cardboard boxes and the empty toilet paper rolls that Housekeeping saved for me. While I was thinking of all these things, Cathy and Cliff were discussing Cate.

"The girl's needing quiet time," Cliff said.

"She took that yesterday," Cathy said. "Unannounced."

"But after the row—"

"She needs to be around people—"

"Depending on the company."

This made me a little uncomfortable, since I roomed with their daughter. Anyway, that was the last word in the argument and Cliff had it, but Cathy didn't budge from her position. Cate was to stay at the lodge and work and I was to have her day off.

"You can go into town, Sarah," Cathy said, turning to me. "It'll do you good after being cooped up for so long in that ice house."

Suddenly Cliff pounded his hand on the outside wall of the lodge. From the corner of my eye I could see the mums in lawn chairs lift their heads to turn and look at us.

"I should have razed the thing years ago," Cliff spat. But as quickly as he'd gotten angry he was suddenly all concern. "Why do you torment yourself, my darling?" he muttered between clenched teeth.

Then, as if he'd forgotten for a moment that I was there, he looked at me with those piercing black eyes and turned and started walking quickly away from us. The mums' heads bent back down to their magazines.

"It's not me who's tormented," Cathy whispered to Cliff's retreating back.

It's awful enough when you're around for a fight between your own parents, but when it's someone else's it's really weird. And when they're your employers it's weirder still. My friend's big sister had never mentioned all this stuff between Cathy and Cliff when she'd told her stories about CC Lodge, and it's not the kind of thing she'd have left out. What could have happened in the last five years? Was it just that Cate was working at the lodge now, too, and that was causing all kinds of stress between them? So who needed Cate working there?

Not me.

Cathy mumbled something about the fact that I could easily get a ride with one of the guests into town, if I wanted to, but that a walk would "probably do me good," and then suddenly I was all alone on the verandah. I could sense that Ellen was looking my way again. She must have been awfully curious about what the scene had been all about, but I wasn't going to give her the satisfaction of me being the one to break the silence and so I pretended to be deep in thought. Actually I was trying to figure out how I could get up to our cabin to get my wallet without going around the pond. I'd have to walk all the way out to the office then back along the footpath, but it would be worth it.

Only when I was coming back again with my wallet did I stop outside the ice house. With all the drama between Cathy and Cliff I'd witnessed lately I had a sudden urge to fling the door open. So I did.

"Begone!" I roared.

Fortunately, there was no one around to see me acting so stupid. Without me in it, the ice house seemed even less inviting. The oars and chairs and things weren't back in yet and the cot and milk crate were still there. And something else. On the milk crate was a notebook and a pen.

Instantly, without even going inside, I knew it was Cate's.

Writing bad poetry, probably.

What would you have done?

It was irresistible. The notebook was red with spiral binding. It had "3 subject notebook, 24.1 cm × 15.2 cm, 300 pages, 3 sections, 200 pages each, college ruled" written on it, but over all that Cate had drawn eyes and lips and noses in black ballpoint pen. Would there be stuff in here about her feelings for Tara? About why she kept disappearing? About me? I took a deep breath and opened it to the first page.

Nothing.

I flipped to the second and third sections and there was nothing there either but, in each of the parts, several pages had been ripped out. Darn. Suddenly I was worried that Cate might turn up at any moment, even though I knew she'd be working down in the kitchen. I put the notebook back, hopefully exactly as it had been left, and got out of the ice house quickly.

TWENTY-ONE

CATHY'S ADVICE WAS GOOD. By the time I'd walked into Gar Harbour I was feeling like I'd had a workout, and my brain certainly needed the oxygen. The thing about the C@P Sites in Cape Breton is that there aren't exactly a lot of computers, and rather than sit and wait for one to be free I decided to grab a bite to eat. I went to the first little beanery, as my dad would call it, that I saw, and who was sitting up at the counter on a stool but Tara? She was so deep in conversation with the old woman beside her that she didn't even notice when I took the stool on the other side. This gave me a good chance to look at the woman. How old would you have to be to have that many wrinkles? Her hair was pure white and pulled up into a high bun and the hands that were wrapped around her coffee cup were huge.

"Well, I'll tell you what, my dear, I worked since I was twelve years old. They put me in cleaning claws and arm meat."

Jeepers. The woman saw me staring at her and then Tara turned to face me.

"Sarah," she said, "I've never seen you in town before. Mrs. Rankin, this is my roommate, Sarah. She works at the lodge too."

Mrs. Rankin had one eye that seemed to be glancing off somewhere else and I always find it hard to know where to look with people like that so I kept my eyes on the bridge of her nose. She gave me the biggest smile with nice straight teeth and I felt a little guilty for being put off by that one eye.

"Well, I'll tell you what, my dears, I feel sorry for the young ones of today growing up. Now, I don't know, maybe I'm wrong."

She was starting to stand when she said this last sentence and she squeezed Tara's arm and gave me another big smile and then she left. She didn't hobble out, either, she was tall and straight and her big hands hung loose at her sides.

"Isn't she amazing?" Tara said.

It was bothering me that Tara had introduced me as just her roommate and not as her friend. This sounds weird, I know, but by being so nice to me throughout my cold, Ellen had kind of cut me off from everyone else. It's hard to explain, but it's like people communicated with me through her.

"Ellen would be able to imitate that wonderful accent."

Why was she mentioning Ellen? On the other hand, why shouldn't she?

"You okay, Sarah?"

"Yeah, sure, just lost in thought. Sorry."

"No need to apologize."

Tara went back to her sandwich and the waitress came over.

"Can I get you something, Dearie?"

"Fries and chocolate milk, please. With gravy. On the fries, I mean."

Well, of course she would know I meant gravy on my fries and not in my chocolate milk. So it wasn't just Cliff who made me act like that. What was it about these people that made me stumble and mumble around them?

"They're so genuine," Tara said.

"Sorry?"

"Well, they're just who they are, that's all. There's no pretense. No veneer."

Had I said all that out loud? I didn't remember saying it out loud. It turns out I'd left out the stumbling and mumbling part.

"You said, 'What is it about these people,' that's all," Tara said. "They're amazing, aren't they?"

"Amazing," I said.

Only I didn't really mean it. I thought they were weird.

The waitress brought my milk and fries. The fries smothered in gravy tasted so good after living on soup and hot lemon. Tara was a little weird too, in that she didn't start talking to fill up the silence that had fallen between us. I thought of how Ellen and I, if she'd been here, would have been laughing about almost everything in the place. It was small—just two tables and three stools at the little counter—and when you were at the counter you could see through to the kitchen, where an old guy with a long grey beard was doing the cooking. He was wearing a red cap and a big white apron over jeans and a denim shirt. The sign out front said, "Simple Honest Food" and I don't think there was anything on the menu that cost more than five dollars. Yet the people sitting at the tables were definitely tourists—having worked at the lodge I could just tell—and there were things scattered around the edges of the room and on the window ledge that were for sale—soaps, knitted booties, and hand made stuff like that. For instance, there were doilies hanging on the wall that were clearly for sale. Doilies. When I pointed this out to Tara, instead of turning it into a routine, as Ellen would have done, she just smiled and nodded.

"Those are Mrs. Rankin's," she said.

When I went over to look at the doilies, which were wrapped in plastic, I couldn't believe my eyes. The biggest one, and it was only about the size of a dinner plate, was priced at one hundred dollars.

"A hundred bucks for a doily?"

Again, if it had been Ellen, she would have run with that, but not Tara.

"It's called tatting," she said. "My mum remembers her great aunt doing it. She used to sew the lace onto her collars and cuffs."

"A hundred bucks?"

"It's a lost art, Sarah. Each doily is made from a single piece of string."

It was hard to imagine those long knobby fingers making all those delicate little knots and swirls from a single piece of string.

"Mrs. Rankin would probably love to teach us if we asked her to."

Whoa. Maybe Tara would be interested in making little lacy knots out of string but it wasn't anything I could see myself spending time on. Even knitting irritates me. One of my mum's friends, when she drops over, always pulls out a bag with her needles and her latest project and starts clicking away. It bugs me. I like to look people in the eye when I'm talking to them.

"I don't think so," I said, immediately feeling that now Tara would be disappointed and not want to be my friend. That turned out not to be the case.

"That was genuine," she said, smiling.

"You done, Dearies?"

We said we were and the waitress took away our plates and brought us our bills. Tara wanted to go to the C@P Site too, but I told her how busy it was and so we walked along the street for awhile. I was dying to ask her about her bio-dad but I didn't know how to raise the subject and I was afraid that I might say something out loud without realizing it, the way I had in the restaurant, so to keep my mind off anything potentially embarrassing I just repeated "left, right, left, right" in my head for every step we took.

How could someone be so uninterested in talking? So many questions were popping into my head, like, did she know where Cate disappeared to? And why? Did she feel Cate had a crush on her? Did she think Ellen had purposely tried to get my job? Had she seen any more of Cliff's wanderings? Left, right, left, right. Did she know if Cate wrote poetry? Had she read any of it? Did she know that on our very first day Cate had been hanging out in the ice house? Did she wonder what Cathy saw in such a grump as Cliff? Left, right, left, right. Suddenly we were standing in front of a window that had "Al's Barbershop" painted on it in white.

"I'm going to get my hair cut," Tara said. "Want to wait?"

Actually, I didn't. But the thought of waiting for my turn at a computer seemed even less inviting than sitting in a barbershop flipping through magazines and waiting for Tara.

"Sure," I said. "I'll wait."

Was I ever glad I did because, while it was true that Tara wasn't much of a talker, she sure was a great listener, and by hanging around with her that day I got to listen too.

TWENTY-TWO

AL'S BARBERSHOP WAS even smaller than the beanery, but it had two barber chairs and five chairs for customers to sit in while they waited for their turn, which tells you something right there. There was no one in the barber chairs, but the other five were filled! Al was actually wearing a white short-sleeved coat—a barber's outfit, I guess, though I'd never seen one before in my life—and he was standing behind one of the empty barber chairs, waving a pair of scissors as he talked.

"Oh, I've seen the world," he said, which made the other five chuckle, then he broke off to look at me and Tara. A little light of recognition glinted in his eyes when he saw Tara.

"Oh, it's the girl from Manitoba," he said and he started pumping the chair to lower it for Tara to climb on. Which she did. One of the men in the other chairs jumped up and gestured for me to take his place. This didn't feel right—he was so much older than me—but then it didn't feel right to refuse, either.

"Oh, don't you worry about Wilfred," Al said as he whipped out a big white bib to put around Tara. "He can perch or he can sprawl."

"Think I'll sprawl," said Wilfred, taking the barber chair beside Tara.

"Excuse me, sorry, excuse me," I said as I made my way past the other four to get to the spot Wilfred had vacated for me. It was such a small shop that unless they'd sat with their legs tucked under their chairs there was no way to get to mine without bumping into their feet on one side or Tara's and Wilfred's on the other. One of the people on my side was a woman and she leaned forward and looked at me and ran a hand through her hair.

"Your friend has a hairdo like mine."

This sent everyone into fits of laughter. Actually, this woman's hair was cropped even shorter than Tara's. I smiled and looked around for something to read while Al started in on Tara's hair. There were exactly two *National Geographics* in a newspaper holder that was nailed to the wall next to my chair. I pulled out one from the nineteen eighties and started flipping through. There was a big section about the woman who lived with the orangutans in Indonesia. Orangutans, apparently, share ninety-nine percent of our DNA. Don't you find that rather hard to believe? Except in the case of guys like Cliff. If you made his hair orange instead of black, added some more weight, and made him hunch over, I think that maybe I'd believe he had quite a lot of orangutan in him. Another burst of laughter brought me back to the barbershop.

"Oh, we didn't know the stove from the table," Al said.

Tara and I made eye contact. If it had been Ellen I'd have crossed my eyes and made some sort of "When can we get out of here?" expression, but it wasn't Ellen. I glanced back down at the magazine but the orangutans just weren't holding my interest. I closed the magazine, put it back in its holder, and was just about to stand and tell Tara that I'd meet her at the C@P Site, when I thought I heard a familiar name mentioned.

"—like those Earnshaws—"

It was Wilfred who'd said it.

Where had I heard that name before? Cliff. *Oh, yes, Miss Earnshaw. Indeed we do.* Cathy's name, before she'd married Cliff, was Earnshaw. I tried to make eye contact with Tara again, but she didn't seem the least bit interested in me. She just sat there, listening, listening, listening to Al and Wilfred. I don't think the content of what they said mattered to Tara at all, it was just being in that little room with those characters that appealed to her. Genuine people having their genuine conversations. Me? I wanted gossip. It made me feel all tingly just knowing I might have information that Ellen didn't. Unfortunately the topic of conversation had switched to, of all crazy things, fairies.

"Oh, he told me where they sat—on the bed, by the table, even *on* the table, all over the place—little people, he called them. 'Hope you treated them right,' I said. Oh, I was teasing, but he was not. He was dead serious as I'm standing here. 'Oh, I gave them biscuits,' he said. 'And along they went after that.'"

"Biscuits?" the woman piped up and it was then that I learned her name.

"It's good that wasn't your biscuits, Betty," the man beside her said, "or it might've angered them."

This made them all laugh again, including Betty, who didn't seem at all offended.

"I'll give you a biscuit," she said, squeezing his knee.

"Oh, I know the score," said Al. "Nobody knows it but the one that was there."

Somehow I had to get the conversation back to "those Earnshaws." But how? They'd moved on from fairies to some guy "down north" who'd picked up a hitchhiker.

"'This is where I get out,' he says to my friend, and out he gets. Then, up ahead, all of a sudden, there he is again, the same guy. 'I picks him up again, on we go. Out he gets again,' my friend says and just down the road a wee bit, what happens?"

"Same fellow again?" Betty guessed.

"The very same."

"What about the Earnshaws?" I blurted out.

Everyone looked at me, even Tara.

"This was Harvey Reid this happened to," Wilfred said.

"Oh, and it happened to an acquaintance of mine in Barra Head, too, same fellow three times—"

"But you said something, earlier, about the Earnshaws."

Now Tara had a little frown line between her eyebrows. I guess it was rude to interrupt Al like that, but if I wasn't careful he'd be off on another story. Was I the only one who knew that Cathy's maiden name was Earnshaw, or was I just the only one who cared? Ellen would have cared, but she wasn't here. If only I could get Al and Betty and Wilfred telling an Earnshaw story then I'd be able to listen and Tara wouldn't be mad at me.

"It's an interesting name," I said. "Earnshaw."

Now Tara had a surprised look on her face, but that was better than a frown, and then I did an awful thing. I fibbed.

"I wonder," I said, "if they spell it the same way my mum spells her maiden name?"

"Oh, there aren't too many Earnshaws on Cape

Breton," Al said. "You'd know. You'd know if your mother was from Meat Cove, my dear."

Meat Cove? Where the heck was that? And what kind of a name was it, anyway? It reminded me of Mrs. Rankin saying they put her in "cleaning claws and arm meat." Yuck.

"I just wondered if you had any stories," I said.

"Plenty of stories," Betty said.

"Plenty of stories about the Earnshaws of Meat Cove," Wilfred said.

"Oh, they were very poor. I know the score. Oh, it was a lot of care."

"No flies stood on that mum."

"Not a one, nope, no flies."

"Then she died and left him with two girls—"

My face felt hot. Would one of those "two girls" be Cathy? I had to just jump in again and ask before they went on and on about "his" grief.

"What were their names? The two girls, I mean."

Tara was looking at me strangely. I guess it did seem odd how I went from being bored stiff to asking for their stories all of a sudden.

"Catherine Elizabeth and Isobel Mae—"

My face was really burning now. Catherine, that would be Cathy, but Isobel...Suddenly I saw Cathy's face in the campfire's light going all tight lipped at the mention of Ellis Bell. Was there any chance that Isobel was the same Isobel that was married to my heartthrob? Then I remembered Ellen telling about that fight where he'd said she "lived in a hovel." But if that were the case, if Cathy and Isobel really were sisters, then her sister was right out there building a house on Only Island! Why wouldn't she go see her? Why wouldn't she say, "Oh, yes, that's my sister"? Why all the secrecy? I just had to ask more, but they were deep into a story about how tough the "old man" (that would be Cathy and Isobel's father) was when he was a little boy.

"Old Doc says it was his first summer, first visit to Meat Cove and he went calling on somebody when a man walked out onto the road, waving his arms. There was he, a little boy of six or seven then, maybe, sitting on a rock beside the road."

"Tough, even then," Betty put in.

"Tough as nails. So Old Doc goes over and has a look. Little fellow's arm comes out and down like this. 'When did he break it?' he asks. 'Oh, about three weeks ago,' comes the answer."

Tara's face looked pained.

"Oh, Old Doc couldn't leave the little fellow like that. Sent the father to get two or three shingles and when he comes back with them Doc made splints. Had to take that little fellow's arm across his knee—"

Tara's face was all squished up like she was feeling what happened next in her own arm.

"Break it, straighten it, splint it and set it up in a sling."

Now Tara was actually rubbing her left arm with her right hand.

"Doc said to bring the boy out in a week's time, but did he?"

"Didn't."

"Never did. Never saw him again for, oh, twenty years, and the arm was that straight and useful."

Jeepers.

"Why did the father wait so long?" Tara asked.

"Cheapness, my dear. You had to pay the doctor in those days so he waited till the new young doctor was down to see someone else anyway and he grabbed him on the road, see?"

"But it could have been—"

"Aye, it could have been months, but lucky for old Earnshaw, it weren't."

"Kid never batted an eyelid, I heard tell."

"That's right, it was pretty much a religion among those folks, even the young children, not admitting to pain."

Jeepers. So that was Cathy's dad, able to stand having his arm broken, twice, without "batting an eyelid," when he was just a little kid. What would he have been like as a grownup? No wonder she could tolerate Cliff, he must seem like a teddy bear compared to her dad. The next thing I knew the conversation had jumped to this generation and they were talking about Edgar (Edgar!), who was obviously from Cape Breton too. According to Al, Edgar wasn't just from Cape Breton, he was "one of those high-and-mighty Lintons." So much was tumbling out so fast and I wondered what Ellen would have made of it all. Now they were talking about Edgar and Cliff.

"Even as lads they had an aversion to each other."

So Cliff and Edgar had known each other when they were young and had married sisters. Cliff had married Cathy and Edgar had married Isobel, and now Edgar and Isobel were living only a few miles away. It was all too weird.

"What would they be needing a whole island for?" Wilfred said, as if he'd read my mind.

They all chuckled.

"A whole island for one month of the year."

"What would old Earnshaw have made of that, eh?"

There was more chuckling and shaking of heads.

"Left those girls well off in the end, though."

"That he did. Lived poor but died rich."

"But he never did acknowledge the child—"

There was complete silence in the barbershop. Tara didn't even seem to notice, she was just looking heartsick and I figured that in her mind she was still back with the little guy having his arm broken for a second time. The names Edgar and Isobel meant nothing to her, of course. But I noticed, and I also noticed Betty's eyes darting towards Al and then Wilfred. They looked a little sheepish.

"Please don't stop," I said. "I like listening to your stories."

"Stories," Betty said, still looking back and forth between Al and Wilfred, "can get old coots into little jimmy-jammies."

Tara seemed to wake up at that point.

"Thanks, Al," she said.

He gave her a mirror then held another one up behind her so she could look at the back of her head. She nodded, then he took a big brush and brushed the clippings from her neck. With a flourish he whipped off the big white bib and he even gave her a little bow as she handed him some cash.

TWENTY-THREE

ONCE WE WERE OUTSIDE I tried to sound light. "So this is what you do on your days off," I said.

"This is what I do," she said.

We didn't talk but just started walking. In my mind I was going over and over the bits of conversation I'd heard in the barbershop, trying to piece it all together. When we got to the C@P Site it had a "closed" sign in the window and a paper clock showing that they'd be open again in one hour. It wasn't long since we'd eaten, so we walked around until we saw a little playground with swings. We sat on them. I really hate playground swings because they have those rubber seats instead of the kind of swing my dad made for me when I was little, with a wooden seat. With a wooden seat you can have one or two people stand and pump while you sit and get a free ride, but the rubber ones just wrap around your bum and leave no room for anyone else to get on with you. Also when you hang from your stomach and twist and twist and then let go and unwind it's not as much fun as a wooden swing.

What has that got to do with anything? Absolutely nothing.

Tara seemed as spaced out as I was from the stories in the barbershop and I was dying to know how much she knew. It seemed to me that she had no idea that Cathy used to be an Earnshaw. I also wondered, since she was so good at listening to people, if she could tell that I'd been lying when I'd said that thing about my mum's maiden name. Now, I hadn't actually said that my mum was an Earnshaw, I'd only said that I wondered if they spelled it the same way my mum did. I mean, there's that game where you tell someone a word like Czechoslovakia and ask, "How do you spell it?" and the answer they're supposed to give is "I-T." Get it? Pretty lame.

Suddenly it hit me. If Tara had no idea that Cathy was an Earnshaw, then none of those stories in the barbershop would have had tremendous significance for her. They were just stories, not about anybody she knew. Only I had that information, so it was safe to do a little questioning.

"You okay?" I asked.

"Yes," she said. "I'm still thinking of that little boy getting his arm broken and how tough those people are."

So I was still the only one who knew about Cathy and Isobel. Wow. First I felt a wave of relief and then, at the next thing she said, my stomach did flip-flops.

"Cate's that tough," she said.

This is what I'd been wanting all morning, to get Tara talking about Cate, and now it was happening without me even trying. I could hardly believe my luck.

"I don't know Cate very well," I said, then added, "I wish I did."

White lie number two.

"I probably shouldn't be talking like this but… you seem to really care for these people. I mean, it was lovely the way you were so interested in their stories back there," said Tara.

I felt like such a fake. Tara twisted around in her swing and let herself slowly unwind, dragging her foot in the sand, before she continued.

"Cate feels there's some deep dark secret about her existence."

"Existence?"

"Mm. She thinks that, maybe, she's not Cliff's… don't tell her I told, will you?"

I crossed my heart and hoped to die, but this was more than I'd bargained for and I felt out of my league. I knew that Tara had a dad and bio-dad but I didn't know if she knew that I knew.

"Would that be so bad?" I asked.

This was the perfect thing to say because then

Tara did tell me about her own situation, which was a tremendous relief because now I wouldn't have to pretend I didn't already know about it.

"So, you must be a big help to Cate, then," I said.

"I'd like to be, but...she just idolizes Cliff so much," Tara said. "I mean, she both wants to know and doesn't want to know. You can understand that."

"Sure, sure," I said, but I was feeling way over my head. I mean, I knew who my parents were because a) I just knew and b) there were the photo albums.

"What about pictures?" I said. "She must have baby pictures."

"No," Tara said. "Not even any pictures of Cathy when she was expecting Cate."

"Well, he doesn't believe in TV or computers, maybe he doesn't believe in taking pictures, either," I said.

"How likely is that, Sarah?"

I had to admit it wasn't very likely, but Cliff seemed so strange to me that anything was possible.

"Why wouldn't they just tell her if she was adopted?"

"Mm, see, my theory is that because he was adopted—"

Cliff was adopted? I could hardly keep all these stories within stories straight in my head.

"Do we know that for sure?" I asked.

"Yes, actually. Cate told me, and I believe her, but also the first time I visited Al and told him I worked at the lodge I got a big story about how Cliff used to live up there."

She stopped and pointed to the mountain top.

Up there? No one could live up there. Was that why he went wandering at night? He was visiting his childhood home? Too weird.

"Not exactly that particular mountain, I don't think, " Tara said. "But one of them. So he lived up there with his family until he was about ten or maybe older and then no one quite knows why he came down, maybe his family got sick or something, but he moved in with some old man who loved him and cared for him and…grew up to be the Cliff we know today."

"Stuff like that just doesn't happen in real life, though, does it?" I asked.

"Well, look at me," Tara said.

"You didn't live up on a mountain, Tara."

"No, but for my whole life I was raised by one dad while my bio-dad lived about ten blocks away. That's pretty strange, too, in a different way."

Whew. A day with Tara was sure different from a day with Ellen. All of a sudden I felt really heavy and saggy, as though someone had handed me a pile of stuff to hold and they'd forgotten to come back and take it from me. What I really should have done, and wish to this day I had done, was get Tara talking more about herself. Instead, I chickened out.

"Know what?" I said. "Maybe all these stories are just stories."

Tara just looked at me.

"I'm serious. I mean, think about Al's stories back there—one was about fairies and the other about some hitchhiking ghost—what makes us think everything else is true?"

"But I was talking about Cate," Tara said.

Whoops. Me and my big mouth. Naturally I'd been thinking about the story about the Earnshaws and trying to piece it all together with this new stuff about Cliff and so my mind was a little jumbled. It's hard to listen and think at the same time. Instead of just stopping and sorting out my thoughts before speaking again, as Tara would have done, I blurted out something stupid.

"Maybe Cate's making this stuff up."

Why on earth did I say that? I didn't believe it for a second. There was a long silence before Tara spoke again.

"Why would she do that?" she asked.

"To make herself sound interesting," I said. "To be dramatic."

"Mm," was all Tara said to that, but it was like a wall had dropped between us.

Walking to the C@P Site, and even once we were inside at our computers, it never occurred to me to lean over and take back my words. First I entered my new password that had nothing to do with Ellis Bell or *Willow Heights* and then I went to my inbox. I wish I had taken a moment to let Tara know that I was just kidding, but I was bursting with information and trying to make sense of everything that was buzzing around in my head. Only when I'd finished a two-and-a-half-page email to my mum about it all did I realize how obsessed I was. I read it over, printed it out, then erased it and wrote simply: *Can't wait to see you guys. Love, Sarah.*

Then I hit "send."

TWENTY-FOUR

WE'D ARRANGED OVER the phone that Mum and Dad would come to pick me up as soon as I got off work, do a little tour, and then they'd take me out to dinner. Though I was happy to see them, for the first time in my life, I didn't quite know what to do with my parents.

At least by the time they visited I was back to working in the daycare and so I could show them that and some of the kids' artwork and stuff. We never bumped into Ellen and that was such a relief. She and I were still fighting, but I knew that if she saw me with my parents she'd stride up and pretend everything between us was normal. Then I'd have to listen and cringe because she goes, like, she goes, ex*cuse* me? hel*lo?* in practically every other sentence. At that moment I realized I'd be embarrassed to introduce her.

Wow.

Could that mean I'd secretly sabotaged the weekend with an argument so I would avoid having her meet the parents?

But she was the one who'd started it by snooping into my email.

But I was the one who'd blown it up into a major fight.

In that way parents have, mine kept saying I could bring a friend along to dinner if I wanted to, but I just kept vaguing them out. Then, as we were driving out of CC Lodge, who was walking at the side of the road but Ellen.

"I know that girl," I said on impulse. "She works at the lodge."

"Let's give her a ride," my dad said, pulling over.

Ellen got in beside me and I introduced her and she told them where she was from and what she did at the lodge and instead of being embarrassing everything felt very nice.

"Want to come to dinner with us?" I blurted out.

"Sure," Ellen said, and that made my parents happy, so everyone was happy.

We drove all the way to Baddeck to a fancy restaurant where there was more than one fork beside the plate and the cloth napkins stuck out of the fancy water glasses. Ellen, who I thought would be a little awkward, seemed the most relaxed of all of us, leaning back in her chair, plucking her napkin and smoothing it on her lap, smiling sweetly at the folks and asking them all sorts of super dull questions that got them talking.

"How was your drive?"

"How do you like camping?"

"Have you driven the Cabot Trail before?"

I sat there, stunned, watching my folks bask in this attention. I thought I was good at handling parents, but Ellen was the master. When my dad launched into a story even I'd never heard before, about a camping trip he'd taken as a kid, Ellen caught my eye and smiled. It was over dessert that she dropped her bombshell, but not the one I was waiting for her to drop.

"So, Mrs. Lock—"

"Carol."

"Carol. I understand you're, like, a huge fan of *Willow Heights*."

I waited for her to say she'd worked for Ellis Bell and then she'd be into it with my mum and then I'd have to tell my mum everything she'd told me, but again Ellen surprised me.

"Yes," my mum said, looking over at me. She was trying to figure out whether I was keeping my own addiction a secret or not. Go, Mum!

"You *know*," Ellen said, leaning forward, "that Edgar Linton has a home here?"

"No," my mum said. "Where?"

And then they talked for around half an hour

about movie stars who had homes in Canada and how little time they must actually spend at those homes and my dad and I talked about movies and books and before long the evening was over and they were dropping us back at the lodge, giving us both hugs and saying they'd be heading off tomorrow morning and what a lovely evening they'd had.

I got a letter from my mum a few days later saying how grown up I seemed and how proud she was and how great it was to be able to share an evening with me like that. Wow. I had done nothing that night but somehow Ellen had us all eating out of her hand and feeling all warm and fuzzy. It was a great lesson in handling parents. Just pretend you're one of those private school kids who ask and answer questions. Normally mum would have sensed when I'd fought with a friend and been after me—"You okay, Hon?"—but there was none of that. It was the most pleasant, phoney evening I've ever spent in my life.

And the best part of it was that Ellen and I were talking again.

TWENTY-FIVE

"CAN YOU be*lieve* it?" Ellen said.

I'd just told her about Catherine Elizabeth and Isobel Mae.

"I'm telling you, they are just so not alike it's not funny. No wonder Cathy got all pinchy-looking when I mentioned my former employer at the cookout."

"Does Isobel look anything like Cathy?" I asked.

"No. Maybe. She's got, like, no thighs, no hips."

Cathy was normal looking.

"Always perfectly made up, you know? Like, just right."

Cathy never wore makeup.

"The hair's always perfectly undone looking."

Cathy pulled hers back into a ponytail or wore it loose most of the time.

"Maybe if you fixed Cathy up—" she said.

"Or left Isobel alone," I said.

"Whatever. Maybe then."

"Anyway, they're not twins or anything, or

people would have said, so there's no reason they should look that much alike."

"There's more," I said.

Ellen's eyes were wide.

"Edgar's from Cape Breton too."

"You're kidding me."

"Nope. They all knew each other and Edgar and Cliff didn't like each other even then."

My stomach was doing flip-flops as I watched her taking all this in.

"And you should have heard how they talked about Isobel and Edgar," I continued, imitating Wilfred as best I could. "'What would they be needing a whole island for?'"

"Well, sure," Ellen said. "The stuck-up dude who comes back to flaunt his success in front of all the little folks back home."

It still stung to hear her talk about Edgar Linton as a "stuck-up dude." As far as I was concerned, the fact that grouchy Cliff didn't like him was a mark in his favour.

For some reason I didn't give Ellen the information that I had about Cate. It just seemed to me that Cate and Ellen hated each other and that Ellen might use the fact that Cate thought she was adopted against her. Besides, I honestly didn't think that Cate really was adopted. She had too many features from each of her parents, including Cliff's temper. Her whole adoption theory was probably just one of those things kids get into when they're feeling blue. When I was eight-and-a-half I was convinced that my real parents were aliens from a superior planet and would be arriving any day to rescue me from Earth.

Ellen and I went over and over everything to get it clear in our heads. She even drew something she called a kinship diagram, like a family tree, showing the men as little squares and the women as little circles. If the man or woman in question was dead now, she put a stroke through their symbol like this: Ø. So Isobel and Cathy were the daughters of some old man named Earnshaw whose wife died when they were young. Cliff was adopted, or, as they said here, "taken in," by an old man. Could that man have been Earnshaw? If so, and if you could believe the stories of people who believed in fairies and ghosts, that Cliff and Cathy (and Isobel) were sort of brother and sister. We both said the next thing at the same time.

"Ewwww!"

After a few minutes of being totally grossed out we both calmed down again. I remembered that my mum's aunt had married her first cousin.

"So that's an actual relative," I said, "whereas, in this case, they're not really related at all."

"Yeah, but…growing up together? In, like, the same house?"

We said it together again.

"Ewwww!"

"No wonder they hire all of us come-from-aways, they don't want locals who know their secrets hanging around."

"No, you think so?"

"Sure. Think of Arvi...she really lives in France, right? Do you ever see her hanging with anyone here?"

"She's too busy," I said.

"Nuff said."

"But all lodges hire people from all over the place, don't they? Think of Jasper and Banff and stuff."

"Sure, but not everybody. You see any able-bodied Cape Breton teenagers in this place?"

I didn't.

"No wonder Cate's a mess," Ellen said.

"You think she's really a mess?"

"Duh, look at her, moping around with her little notebook. I mean, Tara's depressive but she's not, like—"

"Do you really think Tara's depressive?" I interrupted. "She just seems serious and thoughtful to me."

"Uh huh, right. Think what a party cabin we'd have if not for those two sucking the energy down. If it weren't for you and me, it'd be a black hole."

Part of me was very glad not to have a party cabin, but another part of me was flattered.

"When you weren't here? They almost put my little spark right out."

Ellen did an imitation of someone licking their fingers and snuffing a candle, complete with sound effects.

"Fssst."

It was so nice to hear that she liked me so much more than Tara that I told her more of the stuff I'd heard in the barbershop. I actually, and I regret this now, got out my unsent email to my mum and showed it to her.

"'There was complete silence,'" I read aloud, "'when Wilfred said the old man never acknowledged the child. Betty stopped him from saying any more.'"

"'The child.'" Ellen repeated. "Whose child? Isobel's?"

"But Isobel can't have children," I said. "She and Edgar *adopted*."

"So?"

I wasn't getting it.

"Listen, Sarah, people you and I know adopt because they want to have babies. People like *this* adopt because they want to look normal."

Ellen and I almost got in another fight right then. I argued that if Isobel and Edgar had only wanted to look normal, they should have had their own babies (if they could), and that maybe they just wanted to "give back" some of what they'd acquired in life. Ellen said I was still idealizing them.

"Think Arabella," Ellen said. "Would she risk that size-four figure for a baby?"

No. Ellis was always wanting children but Arabella was way too selfish. That's why it was kind of sad that he was surrounded by kids in the pediatric ward all day.

"Hello? Earth to Sarah!"

My mind was spinning. I wish now I'd listened to Ellen (she did sort of know these people after all), because she'd been closer to figuring out the truth than I was, even though I was the one who'd gathered all the information. I was feeling a powerful temptation to tell the secret about Cate's suspicions that she was adopted when Ellen blurted out the idea that got us completely off track.

"Cate has a brother or sister!"

"What?"

She drew a square and a circle, with question marks inside them, beside Cate's circle.

"So if 'the child' is the brother or sister, he or she would probably be around your age, right?"

"Maybe older."

"Well, I can't figure it out."

"Me neither," Ellen said. "We could ask Cathy."

I made a face. I remembered her look when we talked about Ellis Bell. Maybe—and here's where my imagination started to go really crazy—maybe Cathy had been in love with Ellis and Isobel had stolen him and they'd never spoken again since.

"Yeah! And Cathy gets pregnant, and Isobel steals him and Cathy puts it up for adoption without ever telling him."

I could see Cathy not telling Ellis (Edgar, Edgar!). But I couldn't see her putting the baby up for adoption.

"You don't know. She was really young and everybody would be sneering down their noses."

"What would she care? She had money, she could look after him."

"Not *then*, remember? Edgar going, 'You were raised in a hovel' to Isobel. So she and Cathy don't get rich till the old man dies. Maybe he was like, a super-mean old guy—"

I thought of "old Earnshaw" and how he'd had his arm broken by that doctor when he was just a little boy and how he'd shown no pain. My mum and dad are always saying that if you stuff your feelings down they'll come out somehow, eventually. My parents seem to think stuffing feelings down makes you sick, but maybe, in some cases, it just makes you mean.

"—all a little weird around here, you know."

"What?"

"You should've heard Cliff. Some guests are going, 'Oh, it would be so nice to live here year round,' and he makes this snarky remark, he goes, 'Once the tourists leave and the rains come, the suicides start.'"

"That's just Cliff. He says weird things so people will leave him alone."

"Yeah, right, only maybe it's *not* Cliff, maybe he's *not* weird, maybe he's telling the truth and everyone just has their little fantasy of vacation paradise."

This was a recurring theme with Ellen, that underneath everything was misery if you only scratched deep enough. The better something looked, the worse she figured it actually was. And the opposite was also true, apparently—that the worse someone looked, the better they actually were. This sort of applied to Ellen herself, who on first impression was a total joker, life-of-the-party type, when in fact she'd been awfully sweet to me throughout my cold. That's what I thought at first, anyway, then I wondered if she was getting a dig in at me for my "little fantasies" because I like to go off into my head a lot.

I went off into my head with this new information we'd put together, that's for sure. And if it was awkward sharing a cabin with the boss's daughter, it was even more awkward once I had it in my mind that the boss's daughter had an older brother or sister that I knew about and she didn't.

Or did she? After all, Tara knew about her bio-dad. Maybe Cate knew she had a brother out there somewhere. Maybe that's why Cliff was such a grump—he'd wanted a son and had a daughter. Maybe that was why Ellen had seen Cate looking so intensely at Tara, because Tara came from a family where you could know stuff like that and not be all twisted about it, whereas Cliff looked mad all the time. But surely she could talk to her mum? The rest of us kids could talk to Cathy about pretty much anything. But then, she wasn't our mum. And anyway, maybe talking about the son she'd put up for adoption would make Cathy too sad. No one would want to make Cathy sad, not even Cate.

TWENTY-SIX

IN THE NEXT FEW weeks I worked even harder than I had before. The lodge was super busy and even Cliff didn't have time to stand around and scowl at anybody. In fact, I hardly saw Cliff or Cathy at all during that time. One by one the rest of the staff went down with a cold and "Where's Cate?" seemed to be heard even more, not less, so we all had to pitch in and help out in any way possible because the lodge was packed. I was happy to do food prep whenever they asked, and not just because of the extra money added to my paycheque. After a day of being around kids it was great to switch over and listen to the banter in the kitchen. Like I said it's changed my attitude about being a customer forever. In a restaurant everyone occasionally behaves as badly as Cliff behaved all the time.

"Jerk!" Jason said, bursting through the swinging door.

No one responded or anything because he wasn't really talking to anyone in particular; he was just letting off steam. Muttering to himself, really. I kept chopping, the washer kept washing, the cooks kept cooking.

"He wants decaf…I pour him decaf…'this is not decaf,' he says…I show him the orange rim…'This is not decaf'—did one of you make regular in the decaf caraffe?"

No one had. Jason went back to his monologue.

"I make a fresh pot…carry it out…orange rim…pour him a cup…'not decaf' he says. Jerk!"

For a second it looked like Jason would take the decaf carafe and throw it across the kitchen. Fortunately, someone had an idea.

"Water it down."

"What?"

"Tastes too good, add boiling water."

Jason looked like he was past trying to please this guy but after some cursing he poured boiling water into the carafe and headed back out to the dining hall. It must have worked because the next time I saw him he was his usual friendly self.

It can get pretty tense, especially if you're what's called "slammed." That's when all the people come at once to the dining hall instead of spacing themselves out nicely. Cathy said she'd often thought of scheduling two sittings for meals but that it seemed too rigid for their style of family resort. Since people came here to get away from schedules and deadlines, she said, it didn't seem right.

So when you were slammed you just had to get through it and smile a lot and that's when Marsha would be extra solicitous to the people waiting in line. Since they had to be extra smiley on those nights, the wait staff was extra grumpy with us when they came into the kitchen.

"Why aren't my roasted potatoes here?"

"Why isn't the sauce on the side? I said *on the side!*"

"This is medium, I said *rare!*"

And the cooks would get grumpy with everyone.

"You call that fine dice, Sarah? What did you use, a hatchet?"

It made me really nervous at first, but I got used to it because everybody was like that with everybody, not just me. And, when I had to fill in out front, I completely understood.

There was no time to think. It was such a busy night and when Marsha came up to me and said that they were shorthanded and would I fill in at the "front of house," meaning would I wait some tables, I said yes, and the next thing I knew I was borrowing a white shirt and black pants and a nametag that said Andrea that was left over from last summer. I actually thought I wouldn't be too terrible at waiting tables; I'd heard so many stories from the others that I thought I'd be pretty calm about the whole thing. Also I'd seen and heard so much by working in the kitchen. Another motivation was the nice fat sum that would appear on my next paycheque. Still, anything you do for the first time is nerve-wracking.

"Don't sweat it," Marsha said, "you'll be fine. There's hardly any choice tonight, anyway—fish or vegetarian, both with baked potato—and we've only given you three tables."

Only three tables?

Three tables seemed like a whole lot of tables to me. They gave me a little pad with circles around a big circle, representing customers around a table, so that I could write an F or a V in each of the circles and not have to remember who asked for what. As long as I kept smiling and talking to my customers I felt fine, but whenever I looked up and saw the other waiters they seemed to be so much smoother and more confident than I was that it made me shaky. Watching Ellen was amazing. She seemed to just glide around so effortlessly and, I noticed, she didn't talk a lot. Now, because I was nervous, I got all caught up in conversation when I should have been scrambling back to the kitchen or noticing an empty glass or replacing a dropped fork.

There was so much to think about and I tended to focus too much on the people themselves and not enough on serving them and getting on to the next thing. I was standing at one of my tables, deep in conversation, when Ellen glided up and filled their water glasses, something I hadn't even thought to do yet!

"Thanks," I said, when I saw her in the kitchen.

"No prob," she said, and then she was off.

At that particular table sat a bunch of women from New Hampshire. They were very easy to please and seemed to be really enjoying themselves. It had rained heavily that day, their second at the lodge, and as I put a plate down in front of a woman whose hair was done in long cornrows, I chatted.

"Sorry we couldn't provide better weather for you," I said. "Hopefully tomorrow will be clear again."

She looked up at me and fixed me with her sparkling eyes.

"No sense bein' disappointed," she said, "in what the Lord give ya. He give ya what he give ya."

Did she really feel that? What would it be like to go through life so...accepting of stuff? She certainly seemed happy enough, and every now and then there was a burst of laughter from her, and all the women at her table, that made the whole dining hall sound happier.

It was much later that I had an opportunity to talk to Ellen again and then only briefly. I was curious to know how many tables she had.

"Six," she said, then she was gone.

Six? Ellen had six tables and she was still able to notice that no one at mine had any water? How did she do that?

At one of my other tables everyone had asked for the fish, which should have been so easy, right? Except that this one lady, after I put her plate in front of her, looked down at her baked potato for the longest time.

"There's no yogurt," she said. "I want yogurt on my potato."

Before anyone had even arrived we'd put a nice little bowl of sour cream on each table, and a little bowl each of chopped chives and green onions from the herb garden, and a bowl of salsa. But yogurt? No, there was no yogurt.

"I'll get you some," I said in my cheeriest voice.

Back in the kitchen I think I expected to burst through the door and say "Yogurt!" and have a little bowl magically appear for me to take out front, but things were way too busy. So I went to the fridge and found a carton of plain white yogurt, hauled it out, found a little bowl, spooned some into it, and put the carton back—and during this time two other waiters had shouted at me that my tables needed attention. They didn't shout in a mean way, or anything, but just to let me know.

Once I got back to the lady and put the yogurt in front of her I noticed what the waiters who had shouted at me meant. At each of my two other tables there were people trying to get my attention with that eyebrow-raised-head-to-the-side thing or, in the case of one man, the pointer finger beckoning to me. It was just like the first aid course I'd taken for babysitting. I had to decide which was the greater emergency, only in this case instead of choosing between someone bleeding and someone unconscious I had to choose between someone who wanted to order some wine and someone who wanted—what did that man who was crooking his finger like that want? As it turned out I didn't get to choose between those two emergencies, because the yogurt woman was still not satisfied.

"Plain yogurt?" She said it as though I'd brought her a dish of dog kibble or something.

"Pardon?" I said to her, while waving to the guy with the finger.

"I don't want plain yogurt. Don't you have strawberry?"

At that moment I felt like getting Jason's decaf coffee carafe and pouring the contents down her neck.

"Whoever heard of strawberry yogurt on baked potato?" I wanted to say.

But I didn't.

"Of course," I said, picking up the bowl. "I'll be right back."

I could feel the men at the other tables, who'd relaxed a little as they'd thought they'd got my attention, glaring at my back as I went into the kitchen again.

In the fridge there was no big carton of strawberry yogurt, only those little half-cup individual serving containers. After emptying one into a bowl it didn't look like it would be enough, so I went back for two more and emptied those. How much time had I spent on this one woman's stupid baked potato? Yet no one was shouting at me this time to attend to my tables. When I got back out there with the strawberry yogurt I saw why. Whatever the guy with the beckoning finger had wanted, he was tucking into his meal now, and in front of the other one stood Marsha, pouring out a glass of wine. She gave the bottle a little twist so that not a drip spilled and then she set it down and went back to dealing with the lineup. It had to be one of the university students who served wine because we were underage, but how had she known about my table? I sensed that Ellen was looking my way so I glanced at her. She winked, meaning she'd handled the wine issue for me, then went back to serving her own—six—tables.

Somehow I got through the rest of the night.

After dinner, when all the staff were way more relaxed and we were just standing around polishing the cutlery because otherwise it would be spotty from the dishwasher, I would have liked to have talked to some of the others more, but Ellen came over and stayed right beside me. This bugged me. Now that she and I were back to being friends it was like the division between our side of the cabin and Tara and Cate's was even more obvious. How did she do that? I'd had that really nice, if a little heavy, day off with Tara, but now it was almost like Ellen was keeping me for herself again. She started talking, right there in the kitchen, about the whole Cate mystery and it made me feel awkward. She knew it, too, and still kept on doing it.

"No one knows or gives a care what we gab about anyways."

It's anyway, not anyways, but I didn't correct her. And is "gives a care" even an expression? I don't think so.

"I'm not naming names, Sarah Babes," she said when my cheeks were burning their hottest.

She was really bugging me this time. It was one thing to speculate about Cathy and Cliff and Cate in our private talks, but bringing it into the kitchen like that seemed way out of line to me. I just rubbed and rubbed at that cutlery and didn't respond.

"Go, Sarah."

"Thanks for the help."

"Hey, good work tonight."

These were the comments I got from everyone as we closed up and showered and our aching feet dragged us back to our cabins. No one, not even Ellen, was in the mood for a party that night.

"Where's Cate?" she asked Tara when we three were alone and in our pyjamas.

"How would I know?" Tara asked.

"Weren't you the last to see her?"

"What makes you think that?"

You know that game where you try not to make a statement but only ask questions? It was like they were playing it. Part of me wanted to jump in and just stop the game, but part of me wanted to wait and see who won.

Suddenly it hit me, out of the blue, while they were "playing" their game, that Ellen was jealous. I'd had that nice day with Tara and it was during that time with her that I'd learned so much stuff.

When you weren't here? They almost put my little spark right out.

Whereas Tara had been positively friendly with me and Cate was no more surly than she was with anyone else. Hm. It was true that Tara was a little more reserved now that Ellen and I were back to being buddies again, but she was still friendly with me.

Ellen was jealous!

While I was off in my thoughts the two of them had stopped talking and were just staring at each other, both with their arms crossed, both waiting for the other one to say something, so I broke the spell and threw in a question of my own.

"What does it matter?"

"What does it matter?" Tara said, climbing up into her bunk over Cate's empty bed.

"What does it matter?" Ellen said, climbing up into her bunk over mine.

Was that one of those moments where, if only I'd spoken up, the whole summer would have turned out differently? One of those moments where I could have made it clear to Tara that I wanted to be her friend as much as I wanted to be Ellen's? It wouldn't have been at all hard to do except that, the way they were with each other in those final days, it did seem that I couldn't be good friends with both at the same time. I hate having to choose between friends, it's so stupid. Tara was kind and thoughtful and knew tons of stuff. But Ellen knew lots of different kinds of stuff and she was so much fun. For instance, I would never ever have been able to pull off The Caper without Ellen.

What am I saying? I'd never even have imagined it.

TWENTY-SEVEN

THE CAPER REQUIRED some coordinating. We both had to have a whole day off at the same time and, because of me working at the daycare, it had to be a Sunday.

The plan was to infiltrate Only Island.

I get all twisty just remembering. The buzz around Rough Cove was that Ellis Bell and his family were spending all of August on the island. Word got out because of all the things that were being ordered and taken over there. Joanne Dunphy, for example, made more than just muffins for the lodge. She had a home business making cabbage rolls and lasagne for the tourists, and apparently two dozen of her fresh scones were to be delivered to Only Island every morning. Stuff like that. Ellen said it would be a piece of cake to infiltrate because there were always so many people around, even on Sunday, we just had to decide if we wanted to pretend to be personal trainers or flower arrangers. I didn't think I could pull off either of those, and she didn't think it should have anything to do with gardening, so we decided to literally make my dream come true and be window cleaners! Only, Ellen insisted, we had to have funky matching squeegee outfits or we wouldn't blend in. Oh, man.

We called ourselves Window Wizards and we wore high-top sneakers with striped socks. We bought some blue boxer shorts at René's Wear House and put stars and moons on them with the sparkly paint I used for the munchkins. Ellen wanted us to wear halter tops, but I pushed for plain t-shirts with Window Wizards on the back in black sparkly paint. We scored a couple of cheap painter's hats and sewed our own logo over top the Benjamin Moore ad. With a couple of long-handled squeegees from Maintenance and a bucket each, we looked very professional.

"Are we going to actually clean the windows?" I asked.

"No way. We'll maybe have to stand in front of a window and, like, discuss strategy."

"Strategy?"

"Cleaning strategy, like, 'I start top left and work down, you go here,' kinda thing."

A chill went down my back. What if we were caught? I'd die.

"We won't be. And, anyway, so we're caught. So what?"

I felt sick. Jail, fines, public humiliation.

"Even if there *is* some law against walking unarmed onto someone's property—"

"It's called trespassing, Ellen."

"So we're young offenders. You get a trespasser rep for a couple of years then it's wiped. Not to worry. Besides, everyone'll just go, 'Oh, they're so adorable.' I mean, *look* at us."

We did look very cute.

"We're not hurting anyone."

Ellen had a real way of talking me into doing things I wanted to do.

We had to wake up early enough to be out before Tara or Cate. We decided to just slip out of the cabin and dress in the porta-potty, where we'd left our outfits in a backpack the night before. Just as we opened the door I stubbed my toe and yelped. We both stood absolutely still. I thought I heard a sound from Tara, but Cate, miraculously, didn't even stir. It looked like she was sleeping with her head under the pillow, so maybe that helped. I mouthed the word "sorry" to Ellen and she rolled her eyes and we backed out of there very carefully. I felt like I couldn't breathe until we got to the porta-potty.

Ellen changed first, but I could hear her giggling as I stood around in the cold.

"Shhh!"

That stopped her for awhile and then the giggling would start again. Once it was my turn I understood. It's incredibly difficult to change out of jammies and into a phoney costume in the dark in the cold in a porta-potty. You just have to laugh.

"Shhh!" I heard from outside.

I finished dressing with just a few more giggles and since she didn't "shh" me I figured it was because I was so quiet but when I stepped outside I saw that it was because she hadn't been there at all. She was on her way back from the cabin with both of our jackets.

"Good thinking," I whispered. "How did it go?"

"They're dead to the world," she said.

Walking along the Cabot Trail at that hour, just the two of us, the place felt a lot more remote than when we walked into town. There was a point where we could no longer see the lodge behind us and we couldn't yet see the village we were heading to and it was just us two on this winding road in the middle of nowhere. Ellen started walking like a zombie and talking in a zombie voice.

"It's like we're the laaast living cells in a dead baaawdy."

It was funny but it was creepy too.

When we got to the wharf we hung around until seven. The first hurdle, which I hadn't even thought of until we ran up against it, made me think The Caper was over before it had really started, but it turned out to be no problem at all. We walked down to where a few boats were tied and Ellen dropped Marie's name.

"We're supposed to get taken over by…oh, gee…what was his name, Jim, I think?"

"Gary," the guy said and he went away to fetch him for us.

This seemed to me the most incredible bluff, but then Ellen did know these people's ways and she just knew they'd have some guy paid to hang around and ferry "the help", back and forth all day. For a moment I was afraid we'd woken Gary up, but it turned out we'd only interrupted his breakfast.

"Sorry," Ellen said.

"No problem. That's the job," Gary said. "Where you girls from?"

I stiffened. Of course this guy would know we weren't locals. Ellen had an answer in an instant, though.

"We work at the lodge," she said. "We're moonlighting."

He handed us life jackets and climbed into the boat. Ellen sat up with Gary and I just sat behind them and tried to keep breathing. There was no turning back now. I tried to enjoy The View, but it was a little scary. If you looked past the little island that held Ellis Bell there was nothing but ocean until Newfoundland.

"The changes since my grandfather's day, it's unbelievable," Gary said. "When he was young he crossed the Atlantic, over and back, fifteen years—no licence, no ticket, just needed to be able to do the job."

Here we go again, I thought, more talk about how the world's gone downhill. Ellen was nodding away as though she'd lived here all her life and threw in a line she must've heard from Cliff himself.

"Lawyering and lobbying, that's what we've got now."

"That's for sure," said Gary, only it sounded like "Dat's fer shore."

Ellen winked at me as Gary carried on about the old ways and how his father (fodder) knew where he was, "anywhere in the Atlantic," by the colour of the water, the wave patterns, the birds, the seaweed.

"Seaweed?" Ellen shouted above the engine.

"Shore," Gary said.

Apparently his father could gather information from how the seaweed rose or fell below the surface of the water. I looked around me. There was water. There was land. Period.

"He didn't think it out, he just *knew*," said Gary. "Sniffin' the air on a fine day he'd know and sure enough—" shore nuff "—along would come a breeze from the nor'west, just when he'd predicted." Perdicted.

Ellen seemed to be enjoying herself, but my stomach was doing flip flops.

Still, the thought of actually seeing Ellis Bell in the flesh kept me going. And I thought that maybe if we were found out, we only had to go to him and he'd listen to our story and chuckle. He'd probably even agree to having his picture taken with me (I'd bought one of those environmentally unacceptable disposable cameras just in case) and then I'd have a photo of me with his arm around my shoulder, me grinning madly and him smiling kindly. Of course, in this fantasy I was wearing something a little better than my Window Wizard boxer shorts and t-shirt.

Gary said that we could leave our jackets in his boat. He didn't wait around to see if anyone on the island needed to be taken into town, he just helped us out—actually, he helped Ellen then remembered I was there—and headed back immediately. It didn't really seem like the greatest job, but at least he was outside all day. And he'd probably get to meet some TV stars, I mused aloud.

"You kidding?" Ellen said. "For one thing, the stars'll come in chartered float planes. Gary's just for ferrying the likes of you and me and scones, and for another, he could care less."

Couldn't care less, I said to myself, but I didn't say anything; Ellen was still talking as we walked up an incredible winding flagstone path. She suddenly stopped mid-sentence and stood still.

"Holy *house*."

I looked and then it clicked with me what had made her stop. From her description of the house in L.A., this was an exact replica. White, lots of dormers, only there was no hill to build into here so you could tell right away that it was four storeys high. I felt like Dorothy in the *Wizard of Oz* looking up at the Emerald City. Would they even let us in?

"Wayne!" Ellen hissed.

She gripped my arm as if to stop me from going any farther, which I had no intention of doing anyway. There was a man walking around with a clipboard and a peaked cap. Their head gardener from L.A., apparently. Ellen felt there was a slight chance he might recognize her if he talked to her. I felt this meant we were finished and should turn back. Now. But she decided this could work to our advantage. If I would go up to him alone.

"Me?"

"It's perfect, *perfect*. You go, 'You must be Wayne,' and he goes 'Yeah,' and you say you were told Wayne would show you and your partner—" (at this point I was to wave vaguely toward Ellen, who would be turned away from us, holding our squeegees and buckets) "—into the house."

"In? Can't we do out?"

"Look, we'd need scaffolding."

I looked. It was true our squeegees would only reach the first floor windows. Oh, no.

"This is better anyway. We're, like, exclusive indoor window washers. Like those guys who wash only black cars, you know?"

I felt truly vomity as I walked up to this grown man who didn't look as if you could put anything over on him at all. I was certainly glad I'd rejected being a flower arranger with this guy hanging around, because I wouldn't know a begonia from a geranium to save my life. I tried to walk tall. We'd had no trouble with Gary, after all, and at least we knew this man's name.

But it was Ellen who'd pulled that off, and this time it was up to, gulp, me.

TWENTY-EIGHT

IT WORKED! I can't even remember what I said or what he said, but I do remember he never even looked at Ellen. He just took me around to a side entrance and, though I don't remember him actually saying it, I got the distinct impression that we should leave by this same entrance, which was fine by me.

"Piece of cake," Ellen said.

We were standing in a room with a cement floor. My stomach growled.

"You hungry?" she said.

"Don't even think about it."

It was bad enough that I felt like a burglar for sneaking into a person's house, I wasn't about to actually steal their food. Ellen, on the other hand, was calmer than she'd been all day. It was as though once we'd made it inside our problems were solved and we wouldn't be noticed. And since the house was an exact replica of the other one, she knew her way around. I simply would not go with her to the kitchen and, like a little kid having a tantrum, I wouldn't budge as long as she insisted on going, so she left me alone and, after what seemed like ages— during which I imagined she'd been caught and the police had been called and they were searching the house for me and soon a SWAT team would burst through the door—she came back with scones. Joanne Dunphy's scones! The woman in the kitchen had been very nice and had even buttered them for us and given us napkins. They were so good we each wolfed one down before either of us said anything.

"I thought they didn't keep food in the house."

"It's an *island*. Cook's a riot. Used to cater in L.A., but Isobel nabbed her exclusively and now she doesn't even cook anymore, just plans and orders. She said we can have anything we want. Cool, eh?"

This was all too easy. Everyone was so friendly. It crossed my mind that maybe Ellen had just stolen the scones and made up the story about the cook, but I'd had the experience with Wayne. I mean, he didn't go out of his way for me the way they all seemed to do for Ellen, but he never questioned my right to be there.

Ellen's plan was that we should go to the pool and gym area because Ellis was always up before Isobel and he'd probably do laps and have a sauna before working out with his trainer. Isobel would wake up slowly and do yoga stretches in her bedroom before coming down for a swim and sauna. I followed Ellen downstairs and was soon hit with the hot, moist air that was wafting up from the pool area. I was glad there was no one around yet so I could have a good gawk. Now, the only indoor pools I've ever seen in my life have been at recreation centres—big rectangular things, white edges, a ladder at the shallow end, a diving board at the deep end, blue walls. This was nothing like that. This was like an indoor mountain spring, or something. There were rock formations kind of dripping around the edges and right down into the pool itself. We stood looking at it through the glass we were supposed to be cleaning (which looked perfect, by the way, but Ellen said that didn't matter, that the way you kept things looking so perfect was cleaning them even when normal people didn't think they needed cleaning). Here we were down in the basement of the house and it looked like the top of a mountain.

"Those would be fun for the kids," I said, pointing to the rock formations. Ellen nodded.

"Cultured stone," she said.

"What?"

I knew that cultured pearls are pearls that are formed because a human put the little grain of sand in the oyster, rather than waiting for it to happen naturally, but I'd never heard of cultured stone before.

"Fake rocks."

I looked at the sloping formation nearest me. It sure looked real.

"Yeah, but it looks perfect, right? So it's fake."

Her theory again.

"Come on," she said and she beckoned me inside.

There wasn't as much chlorine smell as you'd get at a public pool, but there was an unmistakable whiff in the air.

"Go ahead, lift it," Ellen said, pointing to a rock that was part of a bunch of boulders with water trickling through them and into the main pool.

"I couldn't," I said.

She leaned over and picked it up without even straining. She handed it to me.

"It's…well, it's not exactly light, but…"

"It ain't heavy."

No, it wasn't heavy. I tried to put it back exactly where it had been before. Some of the rocks had a pinky granite tinge and some were dark grey.

"Why would they do fake rocks? There's plenty of rock around here."

She gave me a look as if to say, "How naive can you get?"

"Well, for one thing it's lighter and cheaper, and for another you can make it look the way you want it to look."

It seemed to me that the fun of rocks was that they were a little irregular.

"The path we came up?" Ellen said. "Fake flagstone."

"You're kidding," I said, though when I thought about it, it had been too perfect and smooth in its waviness.

"And ‑upstairs? There's this floor-to-ceiling fireplace made of this stuff so that, like, where there's edges, the rock actually *bends*, get it?"

I didn't. She started doing things with her hands as if that would help to show me.

"Instead of having to fit real rocks together to make a corner, they make a rock that, like, goes *around* a corner. You'll see."

We got some water in our pails and went back outside the glass and tried our hands at actually squeegeeing the windows. Now, this isn't as easy as it looks. I don't mind the spongy part, but it seems to me that no matter how hard you press on the rubbery part it misses somewhere in the middle— like window wipers on the car, where there's always a little filmy swath you can't really see through. I obsessed about this and insisted on trying to get rid of streaks (I didn't feel it was a good idea to actually come and mess up peoples' windows when we were supposed to be cleaning them), but Ellen felt we should just leave it for the real window cleaners, whoever they may be. We were debating this when we heard footsteps on the stairs.

TWENTY-NINE

HIM!

I thought I might toss my cookies, and I actually froze there, holding my squeegee pressed to the glass, aware of his movements behind my back. Ellen was working away, up and down, sponging then flipping her squeegee over and drawing the rubber side from top to bottom. Not until she nudged me with her elbow did I start moving again. I tried to breathe and prepare myself to say "Morning!" in case he said anything to us as he went by.

But he didn't. He opened the glass doors and went in without shouting, "What are you trespassers doing in my house?" or even looking at us as far as I could tell.

I was certainly looking at him. Ellen had to keep nudging me to move my squeegee because lack of movement on our part would be more conspicuous than movement. But it took a lot of effort.

"Not bad, eh?" Ellen said, not even whispering.

He was gorgeous.

A little shorter than I'd imagined, but you

always hear that about stars—especially movie stars, whose noses are about as big as your forearm up there on screen—but so perfect in every way. All fit and toned but not muscle-bound. Long legs, small bum (he was wearing a black Speedo bathing suit). I thought I was going to die. He stood there rubbing his hands through his hair, the way he does when he's got a patient he's feeling helpless about on *Willow Heights*, and then he did a bizarre thing. He must have had it in his hand the whole time, but I hadn't noticed—a bathing cap. A beige bathing cap went on over that gorgeous hair. Oh well. I was momentarily bothered, but then I thought, why shouldn't he protect his hair from the chlorine? No one's watching. At least, not as far as he knew. If we'd been real window washers I suppose we wouldn't have been watching either.

Then he put on the nose thing.

"Sorry," Ellen said, "but those things're *ugly*."

"Shh."

It wasn't so much that I thought she'd be heard, I knew she wouldn't, but I didn't like the "ugly" word used.

"Just breathe out through your nose," she hissed at him through the glass.

It was amazing how much it changed his looks. So I stopped looking. If anyone had tapped me on the shoulder just a few days ago and said that within a week Ellis Bell would be standing in front of me in his bathing suit and I wouldn't want to look at him, I'd have thought they were insane.

Once he was actually swimming I could look again because his head was down.

"Three," Ellen said. She was counting laps. She said he'd do exactly twenty-five laps and then he'd be out and into the sauna. I was actually thinking that since no one had noticed us that must mean we looked like the real thing, so why not interrupt him on the way to the sauna?

"Six."

"Excuse me, Mr. Linton," I could say, "would you mind signing your autograph for me?"

"Ten."

Then once I was deeply into that fantasy it occurred to me it would be much better to catch him after the sauna because he might be irritated trying to sign an autograph when he was all wet from his swim.

"Fourteen."

Besides, he might still have the nose thing on at that point, and I really didn't want to see him with it close up.

"Fifteen."

So then I imagined him coming out of the sauna all dreamy and steamy and when I came to the point where I'm stepping up to him and asking for his autograph I realized that I actually didn't have any paper or a pen on me and he certainly wouldn't because he was just wearing his bathing suit. And what if he didn't wear his bathing suit in the sauna? This was his own home after all. Except that there were always people, like window-cleaning imposters, wandering around it, so that's probably why he'd worn his bathing suit for his morning swim. Except that if he really didn't notice we were there, the way Ellen said he didn't, maybe he would take his suit off in the sauna and there I'd be, asking for his autograph with no pen or paper, and he'd have no clothes on. That would be an amazing instance of my dream "coming true" in an almost-but-not-exact way, because instead of him looking up and seeing me washing the windows in the nude, he'd be in the nude and look up and see a window washer!

"Twenty-five. There you go."

Ellis Bell was climbing out of the pool and, thank heavens, ripping off his cap and the nose thing. He ran one hand through his hair a lot and the other hand had a towel in it that he rubbed over his chest and stomach as he came through the glass doors (I swear he was only about three strides away from me) and then, just as I remembered to breathe, he was already in the sauna. I whispered to Ellen.

"If I could get some paper and pen—"

"You *kidding*?"

Apparently you were never ever to do that.

"We, like, activated the Cloak of Invisibility. Don't blow it now, Babes."

I didn't see that this applied to us as we weren't really working here. I figured I'd had a better gawk than I could have dreamed of and why not try for an autograph to show my mum? But it turned out Ellen had plans for us beyond a mere glimpse of Ellis Bell. She wanted me to see more of how "these people" really were and intended for us to "window clean" most of that day. We gathered up our squeegees and buckets and went looking for more windows upstairs.

So I never did find out if he had his sauna in the nude.

THIRTY

THE CLOAK OF INVISIBILITY only applied to the people who actually lived in the house. The workers, and there were plenty, noticed each other. There was still a lot of painting and building going on in the house and as soon as we got upstairs we could hear the sound of a skill saw, hammering, and all kinds of banging around. The guys would pause, look up and nod, and then just go back to work. The first thing Ellen wanted me to see when we got upstairs was the big fake fireplace, and on the way we passed some painters and I overheard a little snippet of conversation.

"I don't get it, man, what's the point of eleven coats of eggshell white?"

"That's what the lady wants, that's what the lady gets."

"Eleven coats?"

And then they looked at us with slightly worried faces that turned relieved when they realized that we were just more "help" and they turned back to work without any more talking.

The fireplace really was spectacular—floor to ceiling, and in this particular room the ceiling was probably about three normal storeys high—and it really was made of fake stone. Once she pointed out that the corner stones bent around I could tell that myself, but it was amazing how each individual stone looked not only a different shape but a different colour. Lots of dark green and grey and even silvery-looking ones to match the ancient folded rock of Cape Breton itself.

There was absolutely no one in this room so I had a good gawk. The couches (yes, couch*es;* when your living room is the size of this one the usual arrangement of couch, comfy chair and coffee table just doesn't fill the space) were made of cream-coloured material—not leather—and looked like they had never been sat in, and there were tons of pillows thrown on them. The pillows were big too. Everything was big.

The windows were so big and high that I wanted to get out of there because there was no way we could pretend to reach them with our squeegees. Ellen didn't seem to think this mattered at all, but she wanted to leave that room too because she didn't figure anyone would be in it for hours or maybe all day, depending on what Isobel and Ellis did here on the island.

That was a good question. What would they be doing? Would they entertain? If we really hung around all day would we get to crash a Hollywood party? Ellen thought there was a good chance of that, which made me even more nervous because I couldn't imagine myself walking around holding a tray of appetizers wearing my Window Wizards boxer shorts.

"*Dope.* Black and white—just like at the lodge."

But where would we get pants and shirts? Would the caterers arrive with extra clothes? And how would we sneak ourselves past the caterers— wouldn't they know who they'd hired for the evening?

"You worry too much, you know? It's no big deal, I'm not even sure we'll, like, *do* this thing, so don't obsess, okay?"

"But—"

"It happens? We wing it. It doesn't? Then it doesn't. Don't waste all that time worrying."

"But—"

"Sorry I mentioned it."

Then we heard a thump. We both looked up.

"Kids."

Another twist in my stomach. Surely if the kids saw Ellen they would recognize her.

"Outta context? Nah. I'm history."

Still, she moved us into a room off the big room that would have done for anyone else's living room but was apparently the den. The ceilings weren't so high, the furniture was dark brown instead of cream, and this was where there were pictures of Ellis on *Willow Heights* and his two daytime Emmys. I was looking at them and figuring that if someone were to come in I could pretend to be dusting them, when the strangeness of it hit me.

"How come these are here?"

"What?"

"How come he wouldn't leave these at home?"

In seconds Ellen was beside me and picking one up and turning it around in her hands.

"Fake," she said. "Natch."

I held it too. I couldn't tell if it was fake or not, but I must say it didn't seem likely to me that they'd move all the awards and photos here for a month of summer. I mean, if he liked having them around that much then he'd have to pack them up and ship them out again.

"It seems weird," I said.

"There's weird, and there's *weird*," Ellen said, taking the fake Emmy out of my hands and putting it back in its place. "What's it *to* you, Lockwood? It's so important that Edgar Linton be *normal?*"

"No."

I felt like we'd had a fight but I wasn't sure about what. This made me panic because I was pretty dependent on Ellen in that place. If I were to storm off in a huff she would probably stay behind and manage to "wing it," but I didn't have any faith in my own ability to saunter out of there and get Gary to take me back alone without calling attention to our trespassing ways. And I didn't want to leave her to get caught just because I'd chickened out at some point.

It was like when I was in grade six and my best friend stole me a ring that I liked and I, foolishly, went to the store the next day and snuck it back. It only occurred to me after I'd gotten away with it—what if I'd been caught? They'd have assumed I was stealing the ring, not returning it! Then my mum and dad would be called and I know they'd have believed me, but, in coming clean I'd be ratting on my friend—

Where was I?

Oh, yes, dependent on Ellen. It was the way I felt when she wasn't talking to me after I'd chewed her out for getting into my email. I mean, I know my parents were up that weekend so I had other things on my mind and everything, but why didn't I use that non-Ellen time to get to know the others better? I really liked Marsha, for instance—what had stopped me from marching up to her and saying, "I missed you while I was sick." Or better yet, trying to get to know Cate! But no, I spent my time obsessing about whether I was in the wrong to be so mad at Ellen and whether or not we'd make up.

So here's another spot in that summer where I'd just like to turn back the clock and do it again. In my mind's eye I can see me looking at Ellen and saying, "It's been fun but I've had enough," then turning around and just leaving her there. Odds are she'd have come too, but even if she hadn't, so what? I'd have gone down to the wharf and waited for Gary. If someone questioned me I'd just tell the truth—as my Dad's always saying, "If you tell the truth then you don't have to remember what you said"—and see what happened.

But I didn't.

Instead I stuck close to Ellen and so got to see what I'm sure she intended for me to see all along. Not how handsome my heartthrob was, but just how cold he was.

THIRTY-ONE

WE WERE BOTH standing there, looking at the Emmy, me having my Ellen thoughts and her all pulled in and silent, when we heard it.

Crying.

It was in the room directly above us and it was an adult woman, not a kid. You could tell. After listening for a few moments, Ellen whispered, "Isobel."

"How do you know?" I whispered back.

She gave me her most disgusted look as if to say, "Did I not live with these people for almost two months?"

"Maybe it's a nanny, or a massage therapist, or—"

"C'mon," she said, grabbing my arm.

We left the den and crossed through the fake fireplace room. The sounds of hammering and sawing grew louder then softer as I followed Ellen into what was clearly the big entranceway she'd described to me that first night of stories. There was the grand staircase and the mirror and the railings. For a while we'd been out of earshot of the crying, but we could hear it again from here. It was more like sobbing than crying. She'd pause for breath and then the heaving would start again.

Ellen was heading up the stairs, pail and me in hand.

"No!" I whispered, pulling away from her, and this time the look she gave me sent a chill through me.

It was as if she saw that all my protesting was just a show of what I thought was the proper way to behave. The fact is, I wanted to see what was going on. I wanted to spy on Isobel. I was fascinated. It was like those times when I'd been out driving with my mum and dad and we'd pass the scene of an accident and there would be ambulances and police and my mum would say, "Don't look," not to protect me from the shock or anything, but because it's such an awful thing to do, to stare at people who are suffering.

But I always want to. So I stopped pretending and followed Ellen.

She didn't clomp up the stairs, but she didn't tiptoe, either. She was clearly just going to carry on as though she had windows to clean and so I followed her lead.

We turned left at the top of the stairs and down another little offshoot hallway—the crying was very loud now—and there were a bunch of perfect windows to clean. I mean, they were the kind that are broken up into a whole bunch of little panes within one pane so that it wouldn't look at all suspicious to stand there fussing away at them. And if we glanced over our left shoulders, occasionally, there, reflected in a long mirrored cupboard door, was Isobel Linton, with her face in her hands, sobbing.

It was exactly like a car accident. I wanted to stare and I wanted to look away. I don't know how long we were like that before we heard another voice—a woman's voice—but it wasn't very soothing.

"I shouldn't have come."

It was Cathy!

Before I had a chance to register the jolts of adrenaline that were zipping along my arms and spine, or look over at Ellen for confirmation that it was Cathy, she spoke again.

"He shouldn't have told her."

We were so shocked to find Cathy here and yet, when you think about it, they were sisters. It would be way more unusual for Cathy not to visit a sister just a boat trip away, wouldn't it?

Except that when *Willow Heights* was mentioned around the bonfire, that would have been a perfect time to tell us that she was sister-in-law to the hunky Ellis Bell. But she'd gone all tight lipped instead.

Anyway, Isobel was clearly trying to say something, but whatever it was she was crying so much it came out in a horrible wailing sound.

"*Aaoooooh!*"

It was awful to hear. And when I glanced over my shoulder I saw her reflection clutch at her stomach with one hand and double over and pound on the bedspread with the other. She was just like Ellen had described her. Thin, perfectly dressed, hair just right.

It was clear that Cathy was sitting on the bed beside her because I saw the reflection of Cathy's hand reach out to comfort Isobel, but she drew it back without actually touching her.

What had happened between those two that she could make her cry so much and not even be able to squeeze her hand or anything? Cathy was such a huggy person around the lodge. Practically every vacationer got a hug before they left.

But then I thought, maybe this was intentional on Cathy's part—letting her "feel her feelings," as she would have said—because I've noticed that when I'm upset if someone's nice to me then I only try not to cry so much. Then I start that kind of breathing that's rapid and sounds like you're just about to sneeze, only faster, and it goes on and on and you feel like a little kid, which is worse than just feeling rotten. Whatever Cathy's reasoning, after what seemed like an awfully long time, Isobel did stop crying enough to be able to talk again.

She was sitting with both arms around her stomach now, staring down and to the side, sniffling, and her breath heaved occasionally. She had a crumpled handkerchief in her hand that she smoothed out and held to her nose and blew into. Then she went back to clasping herself. Then she started rocking side to side ever so slightly and more and more. Then she started softly singing something that I couldn't make out very well but that sounded like "Lula, lula." When she seemed to have calmed herself again she spoke.

"Why did he do that to us?"

"Us?"

"Dad, I mean."

"Oh, who knows. Who cares." Cathy's words sounded weary and not like questions, but Isobel answered anyway.

"I care. We were raised like…like—"

"We were raised like most of the world still is, Isobel, dirt poor."

"You self-righteous—"

"You self-centered—"

Then Isobel went on about how their father had actually made wads of money on some invention or other, even before their mother died, and never told anyone. So it sat there while the girls "went without."

"…we went without clothes, without shoes, without—"

"Isobel, can we not go over and over this? You and I haven't even seen each other in sixteen years."

"…if not for that I'd have kept the baby—"

So "the child" was Isobel's after all! Ellen and I were exchanging "*aha!*" glances when Cathy cut her sister off again.

"You wanted Edgar, Isobel—"

"I wanted a decent *life*. Not to live in a little shack with no running water…doesn't it ever horrify you, Cathy, that we grew up like that when we could have…the whole time we could have…"

She broke down and cried again.

You know how some people say they're afraid to cry because once they start they'll never stop? I think Isobel must have been one of those people. I'm so used to working with toddlers who bawl their heads off like they're being murdered and then, in the next moment, they're laughing and giggling about something silly. Isobel looked like she could cry for a long time. I was just about to whisper to Ellen that maybe this was a good time to leave when we heard footsteps on the stairs. I didn't need

Ellen to interpret these for me—unhurried, kind of jaunty—I'd already heard them heading down into the pool area.

He must have brushed within a few feet of my back to go into the room where Isobel was and yet there was no comment, no acknowledgment, no recognition that we were even there. I mean, when someone's that close you think you'd at least say, "Excuse me, we need a little privacy—could you work somewhere else?" But it was just like Ellen said—we were invisible, ghosts, wallpaper.

My stomach didn't even flip-flop.

THIRTY-TWO

"WELL, CATHY EARNSHAW, this is a surprise. Welcome to our humble abode." He bowed slightly.

"I didn't come to see you."

"Lovely, as ever."

"And it's Heath."

"Of course, Mrs. Heath. How is old Cliff? Still around to cause trouble or has he walked back into the bogs yet?"

"If you were half the man he is—"

I could just imagine Cathy looking right at him with her intense eyes and saying that.

"Oh, stop it, you two."

This was from Isobel. She said it as though they'd picked up in the middle of an old fight, but she said it so weakly that neither of them paid any attention to her. So she said it again.

"Just stop it."

And this time Edgar (I had stopped thinking of him as Ellis from the first words he'd spoken) looked over at her, briefly, before looking back to Cathy.

"You've upset my little wife."

"Don't think for one second that's it's my presence here and not your indifference to her anguish that torments Isobel."

At this point Isobel lay back on the bed with another one of her awful sounds.

"*Ohhh*," she groaned, rolling over and burying her face in her hands.

Neither Edgar nor Cathy seemed to notice.

Cathy moved in closer so that she was standing over Isobel, glaring at Edgar. Edgar stood on the opposite side of the bed. Cathy was sort of sticking her head forward slightly. It looked like she was getting ready to haul off and hit Edgar, but he was just standing there with his hands on his hips or sometimes folded, as though he were observing the whole thing, like us, instead of being part of it.

"You cold, scheming, vicious—"

"Cold *and* vicious? Bit contradictory, that."

"Not at all! 'Motivated by ill will or spite'— that's you, Edgar. But if you'd ever studied more than how to look bland before a camera you'd have known that."

"I wouldn't lord your grade ten education over me, Miss Earnshaw—"

There was another groan from the bed but neither of them paid any attention to it. My head was spinning so fast I couldn't keep up.

"—just because you bought yourself a job with your money—"

"And my sister bought herself a husband—"

More groaning.

"She certainly got the better deal."

He looked so pleased with himself that I was ashamed of ever having thought he was the living end.

"I hate you."

Those words, which look so strong on paper, were said in a weak little voice by Isobel who hadn't even raised her head to say them.

"To whom is she speaking, do you think, Catherine? *Toi ou moi?*"

This time Isobel did turn over and push herself up, but since she was crying again the words didn't exactly come spitting out of her the way they had out of Cathy.

"You. You have actually succeeded in making me hate you."

"Have I? Are you sure, Isobel? Don't you like shopping on Rodeo Drive? Sitting next to directors' wives while you get your hair done?"

He walked over to one of the big windows.

"Look there. Look at where you started, where, but for me, you would still be. Go ahead. Go back to all those people who hate you, and the child you abandoned who, if she knew you, would hate you too."

It gave me a chill to hear him talk so coldly about the adoption. And now we knew the baby had been a girl. Before I had time to think about this, though, Edgar was speaking again.

"Perhaps C and C would take you in. You could work for them, Isobel. Help around the lodge, hm?"

I wanted to hit him.

THIRTY-THREE

JUST AT THE HEIGHT of all this awful stuff—
Isobel was crying again, Cathy was spitting
something in anger, Edgar was looking bored—
who should run into the hallway but little Belle?

Our automatic reaction was to turn our heads
towards her, but she just froze in her steps a few
feet away from us, listening. Ellen had time to turn
her head away again, which was good, because
unlike her parents, Belle noticed us.

She looked right at me. She had two black
pigtails and she was wearing coverall jeans and a
t-shirt. She was such a tough-looking little kid that
I expected her to swear any moment, but then—I'll
never forget this—her face just crumpled. It was
the weirdest thing. She wasn't making any noise at
all, but her face was all squished up as though she
were crying loudly. I nudged Ellen who, it turned
out, was already watching the silent sob. Then Belle
clenched her little fists and stood rigid like that for
awhile, her face still all squished, and suddenly she
turned on her heels and took off.

Amazingly, Ellen followed.

Now what was I supposed to do? I guess I should have followed Ellen and Belle, but since I didn't do that on impulse I became immediately aware of the argument in the bedroom reaching its peak.

"Do it, Isobel," Cathy was saying through clenched teeth. "Come with me now."

"That's right, Isobel, go back with your big sister and Cliff. It'll be just like old times, won't it? The three of you there—not quite as crowded as the hovel, but crowded—"

"Shut up," Cathy said.

"Look, sister Catherine. She's not remotely interested in following you."

"I—"

"Leave all this?"

He held his hands out and looked around.

"She couldn't if she wanted to. And, believe me, she doesn't want to."

"Leave him," Cathy said to Isobel, and Isobel looked as startled as if she'd been hit. But she didn't say anything. She seemed to have no energy.

Except she had enough energy to get up off the bed, slip her arm through Edgar's, and walk out of the bedroom with him.

I felt them moving behind me. I felt Cathy, standing in the bedroom.

I just wanted to evaporate, but after waiting as long as I possibly could to be sure that Edgar and Isobel were gone, I picked up my pail and Ellen's pail and put our squeegees under my right armpit and went to find her. I figured she and Belle had gone to the kids' floor, which was up one flight of stairs and, after Ellen's stories, a piece of cake to find. It was impossible not to catch a glimpse of myself in that big mirror like the one Edgar had stopped in front of when he should have been running to find out if his son was dead or not. I stopped in front of it too.

The ridiculousness of my outfit and the squeegees isn't what made me stop, it was my face. I'm always teasing my mum about her "worried face." I hate it, actually, the little inverted U she gets on her chin when she's fussing over me. The line between the eyebrows. There they were. On me. I broke into a goofy grin just to try and stretch those lines away, and it worked, but it didn't really matter because I'd seen them and I knew my face could snap back to that when I wasn't looking. Ugh.

I tried Eddie's room first. No one there, but I dropped the pails and squeegees and went to Belle's room.

There the three of them were, sitting on Belle's ridiculous princess bed, Ellen in the middle with a sad little kid on either side of her and an arm around each of them.

"It's okay," she kept saying softly, giving them little squeezes. "It's gonna be okay."

Oh yeah? I thought. Tell me another one.

THIRTY-FOUR

ELLEN SAID SHE WASN'T leaving the kids, and since I didn't know them at all and felt like a fifth wheel in that room, I just turned around and walked down the stairs and out the front door, not even the side entrance. By this time I really didn't care about getting caught, and naturally when you don't care nothing happens.

Gary helped me into the boat and asked after the missing Ellen.

"More work to do," I said and he shrugged.

It was a little odd, I guess. One Window Wizard and not a squeegee in sight. But he just handed me my jacket and life jacket and started across. He made a few attempts at small talk but I just answered yes or no and so he gave up and we didn't talk at all on the crossing.

It wasn't until we reached the other side and I started walking that I realized how tired I was. Bone tired. I managed to climb up to the highway, but I think I could have stretched out in the middle of the road and slept and not cared what people thought or whether my mouth dropped open while I was lying there. I was wondering if I had the guts to stop a family and ask for a lift, the way Ellen would have done, when I looked down the road and saw a familiar truck. Cliff was driving it. Even though he was pretty far away I could tell he was mad. He pulled over, got out, slammed the door, and, without looking left or right, strode across the road to my side. I felt like a bug caught in a jar.

"Where is she?"

He stood there, his eyes wild, his hair wild, looking crazy. Crazy and dangerous.

"Where is she?" he roared again.

I assumed he meant Cathy. "There," I blurted out.

He turned, as I spoke, to look at Only Island. It was a look of pure hatred.

"The child wants her natural mother, that I understand, but if she chooses to live with that… that…sorry excuse for a man—"

What on earth was he talking about? I'd have asked him if he weren't so scary. Suddenly he turned on me.

"It's you! You and that wise-cracking army brat who've brought this about."

He grabbed me by the shoulders.

"What? Brought what about?"

"Poking your noses into our business."

He jerked his head in the direction of Gar Harbour, but he still had a grip on my shoulders and hatred in his eyes.

"I'm sorry—" I started to say, but he cut me off.

"Sorry? Sorry's not enough. Sorry—is that what you say when you've—is it?"

He was shaking me by the shoulders and shouting. The veins on his neck were popping out and his teeth were clenched. I was terrified of him. Suddenly a car pulled over onto the shoulder near us.

"Y'all okay here?"

I'm sure by the look on our faces the woman in the passenger seat knew we were not okay.

"Can we give you a lift, honey?"

"Yes!" Cliff growled.

He grabbed me by the upper arm and opened the back door to the car and shoved me in and then slammed the door shut. I burst into tears as the man who was driving pulled back onto the highway.

"You know, I don't care what you've done," the woman said, "your daddy ought not to rough you up like that. It's just not right."

"He's...not...my...dad," I sobbed.

THIRTY-FIVE

WHAT ON EARTH had just happened? Why was Cliff in such a rage at Ellen and me?

The nice couple didn't want to just drop me at CC Lodge and leave me alone. They were driving to Sydney to catch the ferry to Newfoundland and I think that they'd have taken me with them if they could rather than have left me there! I had to calm down and stop crying just to prove to them that I was going to be okay. We sat in the parking lot for a while. The man occasionally glanced at his watch and every time he did that his wife shot him a look.

"I'm not leavin' till I know who's lookin' out for y'all," she said.

Fortunately, I saw Arvi heading for the office and so I rolled down the window and called to her. She came over looking all concerned and motherly and I could sense the woman relaxing a little. I got out of the car.

"Oh, Sarah, I'm so glad you're back."

Arvi threw her arms around me and gave me a

big hug, which was the first time she'd ever done that.

"I was afraid you had run away also!"

Also?

It was on the tip of my tongue to tell Arvi that Ellen and I hadn't run away, we were just poking our noses where they didn't belong, when it occurred to me that it was our day off together, after all, and why was she being so hysterical about us being away on our day off? The nice woman had gotten out of her car by this time and was standing beside us.

"Now who all would blame this girl for runnin' away? You should have seen how that brute manhandled her."

Arvi held me away from her and looked into my face. "Goodness me, dear Sarah, did someone harm you?" she asked.

"No," I said.

"Yes, indeedy," said the woman.

"Now, Cora," said the man's voice from inside the car. "We have a ferry to—"

"Hush, Merv, this girl here's been traumatized and I'm going nowhere till I know she's taken care of."

"Please," I said, "don't worry about me." Then I turned back to Arvi who was still holding me by the shoulders. "This nice woman and her husband saw Cliff getting mad at me—"

"Mad? Honey, I've seen mad. That was a crazy person."

Arvi took her hands away from my shoulders and buried her face in them. Then she clasped her hands together in front of her and moved them up and down as she talked to the woman.

"Please, dear lady, do not be alarmed. Mister was very very upset because his daughter has run away, you see."

Only once Cora and Merv were on their way again, with many thanks from me and Arvi, did it really hit me that this wasn't just one of Cate's typical disappearances, that she had actually run away from home. That's what Cliff had meant when he'd wildly asked, "Where is she?" *Where is Cate*, not *where is Cathy*.

Apparently after breakfast was over and Cate, once again, hadn't shown up for her shift, the kitchen staff's irritation with her grew and grew. Usually Cathy handled it somehow, but Cathy wasn't around. When Tara said that Cate was still asleep, Arvi went up to our cabin and found all three of us gone and a note from Cate saying she'd run away for good. Then Cliff had stormed off and the whole lodge was in turmoil. It was as though no one knew what to do or how to behave without Cathy there to tell us.

Instead of Arvi asking, "Where's Cate?" everyone was asking Arvi, "Where's Cathy?"

Arvi didn't know. Only I knew. Did I tell? I wanted to, it was on the tip of my tongue, but I stopped myself. God knows there had been plenty of opportunities for Cathy to point to the island and say, "My sister is there," if she'd wanted to, but she never had and I wasn't about to reveal anything. I could just imagine the questions everyone would have about her glamorous sister and brother-in-law.

As if it weren't enough to have The Caper end so disastrously and to have Cliff so furious, Tara was very cool with me. Who could blame her? She'd woken up to three bunks all made up to look as though the sleepers were still there. No wonder Ellen and I had had no trouble sneaking out early in the morning, Cate had already snuck out and only Tara was left! She'd tiptoed around, knowing that it was our day off and that Cate wasn't needed till later, so that we three could sleep in. But there was more to it than that.

"Your exhaustive research into local history was fascinating, Sarah."

"What?"

Though I pretended not to know what she was talking about, I knew exactly what she was referring to—my unsent email to Mum.

"Mm. Cate showed it to me."

I felt awful. Then a little self-righteous. What was Cate doing poking around my stuff anyway?

Then I felt sick again as I remembered looking at her notebook in the ice house in the hope of finding some of her sad poetry. Of course Cate would read my letter, if she'd found it. I would have read hers.

How had she found it, though? Had she snooped, or had Ellen "accidentally" been seen reading it and then stuffing it away when she came in? I'd never know now. I only knew that I felt rotten for my part in the whole thing.

Tara could tell I was sincerely sorry, but she still didn't want to go over any of the details with me, she wasn't that kind of person, and I didn't want to seem even worse in her eyes than I already did by asking just how much Cate had figured out on her own and how much she'd gotten from my letter.

As soon as she got back to the lodge, Cathy called a meeting. We all gathered in the dining hall. Here's what she said.

"I'm afraid I have to ask you all to pitch in even harder for this last week of the summer as we've lost two workers—three, really, as Cliff has gone looking for his—" she glanced over at me, "for our daughter. I'll take Ellen's shifts myself. Todd, Hilary, and Bethany, I've scheduled the three of you to cover Cate's kitchen duties."

Cathy really was amazing. She was so calm and in control and because of that my heart stopped pounding. Everyone gave her a hug after her talk and when it was my turn I wondered if she'd give me a special look or anything like that but she didn't and, I guess, why would she? She didn't know that we'd overheard her fight—we'd put on the Cloak of Invisibility. She maybe didn't even know that Ellen was still on the island! Why would she? My bet is that after I'd gotten into the car with the nice couple, Cliff had gone down to the wharf and met Cathy coming back from the island and realized that Cate hadn't gone there after all. Then he'd taken off after her. I was so relieved to hear he was gone, because I was scared of him, that it was only later that I put two and two together myself.

On my very first day at the lodge Cate had shut herself into the ice house and Marsha had inadvertently invaded her privacy. Maybe she was writing sad poetry, but maybe she was just getting away by herself to think about things. It was Ellen who had put the sad poetry idea in my head. Ellen and Cate had become immediately antagonistic at the first bonfire and, because I was feeling lonely and isolated myself, I gravitated towards Ellen as a friend. She seemed so much more easy and at home in the world than the rest of us. She *is* more easy and at home in the world than the rest of us. But that meant that Cate perceived me as antagonistic towards her too—which, okay, let's be honest, I was. She seemed like a carbon copy of her grumpy dad. Then I took over the ice house. I didn't do that intentionally, but Cate would have perceived it as another invasion of privacy.

Tell him—no, I'll tell him—it was Cate's idea.

Probably Cate did complain about my disturbing her sleep, but she would never have suggested that they put me in "her" ice house. And, here's the big thing, she was probably listening and *did* hear me and Ellen talking about her that time. It probably *was* her who had slammed the door shut, not the wind. Ellen had certainly thought so.

You'll have to push harder next time.

And didn't Cate's disappearances start to get worse around that time? I seemed to recall that the first time she took off for a whole afternoon was the day I'd been set up in the ice house. So first I take her hideout, then she hears me gossiping about her. Yes, and the more Ellen and I found out, the worse her disappearances got. It was like she, and we, were tracking along some parallel path of discovery—her talking with Tara about adoption and bio-dads and stuff that was real, us going over and over stories about Edgar and Isobel or focussing on Cathy and Cliff and their strange mix of passion and calm, grumpy and soothing—until our paths crossed and she'd read my email.

She'd read my email. The email, I now realized, that was filled with speculation and half-truths.

Had Cate figured it out, too? Of course. That's why she'd run away. Figuring it out myself, I could understand why. I remembered that night when I saw Cliff banging his head against the tree and Cathy ran out and seemed to be comforting him. It was so un-Cliff, or so I thought at the time. That's not the way people who are angry at other people behave, it's the way people who are angry at themselves behave. Wasn't that exactly what Cathy had whispered on the porch as he'd walked away the next day?

It's not me who's tormented.

Everything finally started to come together in my head.

"Cliff has gone looking for his—for our daughter," Cathy had said. Then she'd given me one of her looks. I remembered her voice in Isobel's bedroom saying, "He shouldn't have told her."

Cliff had told Cate something and that's why she'd run away. Then he'd gone looking for his daughter, not their daughter.

The child wants her natural mother, that I understand, but if she chooses to live with that…that…

Suddenly it all made sense. My friend's big sister never mentioned how grumpy Cliff was because he hadn't been then. He was probably just "genuine," to use Tara's word. The grumpiness may have started when Edgar and Isobel bought Only Island, or it may have begun when Cate started to have suspicions about being adopted. There *was* a secret around Cate's birth, but it wasn't that she'd been adopted. She'd probably confronted her folks with my email and they'd told her everything, including the fact (and it only occurred to me in that moment) that she'd been conceived in the ice house she felt so drawn to. Ellen had been right that day I'd told her all my information. "The child" old Earnshaw never acknowledged was the baby that *Isobel* had given up—before her father had died and she and Cathy discovered they weren't actually poor—and wasn't even Edgar Linton's. *I♥C* didn't mean *I love Cliff*, or even *I love Cathy*, it meant *Isobel loves Cliff*. Cate didn't have a dad and a bio-dad, she had a mum and a bio-mum.

Cate was Cliff and Isobel's daughter.

THIRTY-SIX

I WORKED MY BUNS off that last week. I was trying not to think, to keep so busy and work so hard, that I'd fall into bed exhausted. I "pitched in" way more than was normal. I helped clean and vacuum the rooms, I polished cutlery, I cleaned and refilled salt and pepper shakers, I even weeded the rock garden. I hate weeding. Then there was my regular job with the munchkins, which had lost a lot of its appeal. I would just look at all those little kids—especially the overly quiet ones, the ones twisting their little stuffed animals, or pulling their hands up into their sleeves—and wonder what was going on in their heads. To them I was almost the same as an adult. Did they have any idea how messed up adults were? How could they?

I just wanted to go home. I called my parents and asked them to pick me up the very minute my last shift was finished. I didn't even go to the farewell bonfire. I'd never have believed it if someone had said at the beginning of the summer that I'd be so happy to drive away from CC Lodge.

My parents had "saved" the rest of the Cabot Trail to drive with me so as soon as we hit the National Park it was new territory for all of us. At the top of the first big grade we climbed there was a lookoff and my dad pulled over. A van with a family in it was parked there too, and my dad asked the man if he'd take our picture. When I look at that photograph now, I see my mum and dad smiling into the camera, but my eyes look as if I just want to get away from there. Behind us you can see the twists and turns of the trail, the green-covered mountains on one side and on the other an island out in the grey ocean. Only Island. People always look at that photo and say how beautiful it is.

As we got back into the car I thought of Ellen. What made her feel ready to make a decision to stay like that? Sure she was older than me and ready to move on to the next phase in her life anyway, but…what a decision to make. I'd known when I looked into her eyes that she really wasn't going to leave Belle and Eddie again, and, knowing Ellen, she'd get her way and whatever money, holidays, clothing allowance, and manicures she felt a proper year-round nanny deserved.

What would it be like for her, I wondered. Then I remembered the time last summer when Mum and Dad and I had driven to Fredericton and were wandering around. It was a terribly hot day and we were all in bad moods. Coming down the street towards us we'd seen the first person of the day who looked truly happy and even my mum commented on it. It was a woman pushing this young guy in a wheelchair. I don't know what his condition was, but his legs were all wasted and his hands flopped in front of him and his head lolled to the side. But he had a big grin on his face, and her face, the woman pushing, I mean, was positively beaming. I'd never seen anyone look that happy before or since. Until Ellen. Sitting on the bed, with a sad little kid on either side of her, she looked that happy.

So crazy old "Gandhi," "anyways," "she goes, she goes, and I go" Ellen is going to stay with those awful people and make sure her little Bulmanians get taken care of. I'm the one who knows the whole story, but she's the one who's amazing. To think that she felt ready to commit herself like that.

I'm kind of jealous.

I didn't tell my folks anything about all this, so they have no idea that CC Lodge doesn't interest me anymore. For instance, now that he recognizes the name my dad will see a letter to the editor in *The Globe and Mail* or *Maclean's* by Catherine Heath and he'll read it aloud and say, "Very thoughtful. Very intelligent," or hand it on to me to read. But it doesn't matter to me anymore that Cathy's insightful or articulate or that she and Cliff run an ecologically desirable resort or that the CAA rated it among the top ten family destinations in Canada. Just hearing the name CC Lodge brings up an image of Cliff's tormented face and the anger and sadness that is inside Cathy but that she keeps hidden.

When I got home it was clear, though, that all my interest in *Willow Heights* had just disappeared. Gone. Will Hermione ever get Ellis? Will Mark reconcile with his parents before he dies? I couldn't care less. Or, as Ellen would have said, all wrong but with so much feeling that she'd have gotten it right, I could care *less*.

I was gearing myself up to tell my mum that I wouldn't be doing Sunday morning gorge-fests anymore. It felt a little like the time I had to tell her I wanted to stop taking piano lessons, like it would be a huge disappointment. That time it had been, but this time it wasn't. It turned out that over the summer, she said, she'd realized that what she really liked was spending the morning with me. Plus, while I was away, she and Dad had discovered this little restaurant in an old house out in the country where you could get a great greasy breakfast and endless coffee. So what happens now, on Sunday mornings, is Mum and I sleep in while Dad goes for the Sunday long run, then we wake up and drive to the restaurant and meet him there and we all pig out together. He likes it because he gets to run point to point instead of looping back to the house, she likes it because she still gets to spend the morning with me, and I like it because I know that when I'm grown and gone they'll continue the routine and have just as much fun without me.

No, all that remained of *Willow Heights* for me was the trees themselves, which are after all very pretty, and for some reason, after I got back, I found myself going to that stand of them that I'd tried to make out under in grade seven. I'd just go and be there in the middle of them and enjoy the swaying of their branches and their bigness and oldness. In November, when the maples are bare and the willows still have their leaves and they've turned yield-sign-yellow, I liked to go and stand there with just a dusting of snow on the ground and look out at the world through those drooping leaves.

I say *liked*, as in past tense, because there was a big ice storm and when I went to the willows for the first time after that there were a couple of men with chainsaws and a township truck. It seems that what with the weight of the ice and the strength of the wind they just lifted up and keeled over, all three of them, like dominoes. Shallow roots.

So now I have nothing but memories. Memories of a great and awful summer. And now instead of looking at grown women and seeing little girls, I look at little girls and try to see what kind of grown women they'll be. At what point will they get their permanently set mouths, frown lines and put-upon faces? When exactly does it happen? I don't want to be one of those bitter old ladies looking out at everybody as though everybody irritates them. When exactly does it start?

The worst part is thinking of Cate. She already had her tight face, and no wonder. She's going through life with this thing hanging over her head. I can't bear the fact that my need for gossip and excitement prevented me from getting to know and maybe even help her. She's out there somewhere with all that hurt building up inside her.

Tara, you're the sensible one, the earthy one, the one who's going to travel. The one with a mum, a dad, and a bio-dad. Maybe someday you'll meet up with her again. Will you fix it for me? Tell her I didn't mean to be so stupid. Will you do that? I see her sad face all the time and I can't bear it hanging there in my mind.

She haunts my dreams.